3 932

D1013831

Intrigue at the Raft

B O O K   O N E

Intrigue at the Rafter B Ranch

S T E P H E N   B L Y

CROSSWAY BOOKS • WHEATON, ILLINOIS
A DIVISION OF GOOD NEWS PUBLISHERS

Intrigue at the Rafter B Ranch

Copyright © 1997 by Stephen Bly

Published by Crossway Books
          a division of Good News Publishers
          1300 Crescent Street
          Wheaton, Illinois 60187

Cover illustration: Sergio Giovine

Cover design: Cindy Kiple

First printing, 1997

Printed in the United States of America

Library of Congress Cataloging-in-Publication Data
Bly, Stephen A., 1944-
    Intrigue at the Rafter B Ranch / Stephen Bly.
       p.   cm.—(The Lewis & Clark Squad adventure series ; bk. 1)
    Summary: While discovering how to be a real team under the guidance of a new basketball coach, four friends investigate strange happenings in a prairie pasture and trust in the Lord to lead them.
    ISBN 0-89107-939-4
    [1. Basketball—Fiction. 2. Christian life—Fiction. 3. Mystery and detective stories.] I. Title. II. Series: Bly, Stephen A.,
1944-   Lewis & Clark Squad adventure series ; bk. 1.
PZ7.B6275In 1997
[Fic]—dc21   96-40083

05	04	03	02	01	00	99	98	97
15	14	13	12	11	10	9	8	7	6	5	4	3	2	1

For my good pal
Lindsay "Tex" Ailor

One

🏀

*F*olks, you ought to be here! The crowd is going absolutely wild! Trailing by seventeen points early in the fourth quarter, the Halt High School Huskies have battled back to tie this Idaho State Championship game with only six seconds left to go. Most of the points have been scored by incredible baseline shots and two—no, three slam dunks by the Huskies' tall, strong senior, Cody Clark.

The Wildcats have the ball; Heatherton inbounds the ball to Tony—No! Clark steals the ball and breaks down court! Baby, he's going all the way! 5-4-3-2—and he reverse slams it at the buzzer! It counts! The Huskies win the championship! The Huskies win the championship!

The crowd is thundering, "Co—dy! Co—dy! Co—dy!"

Yeah . . . sure.

Cody Clark sat on the first row of the bleachers and tied his black basketball shoes.

"Does Nike still make those?"

He glanced up to see his new neighbor standing in front of him, pointing at his shoes.

"They used to belong to one of my brothers."

"You have more than one brother?" Larry asked as he dribbled a basketball.

"Yeah, Prescott and Reno are out on their own. These shoes used to be Denver's. He's the one in high school. I guess his feet grew fast, and the shoes never had much wear. Figured I might as well save myself some money."

Larry dribbled back and forth between his legs. His voice sounded high-pitched and nervous. "You mean you buy your own basketball shoes?"

"Yeah. Don't you?" Cody ran his fingers through his shaggy brown hair and stretched his legs out onto the basketball court.

"Are you kidding? These suckers cost $134.50, and that's the discount rate my dad gets. You figure that times three, and there's no way I can come up with money like that."

"Times three?"

"I need a pair for indoor games, another just for outdoor games, and a third for practice. So how in the world would I make over $400?"

Cody shrugged. "Work?"

"Hey, I'm just barely thirteen."

"So am I, and I work."

"Sure, but your folks have a farm. That's different."

"A ranch, not a farm."

"Yeah, whatever." Larry's bright blues eyes danced in rhythm to his dribbling. "Hey, did you see my move to the basket on the tall guy who's going into high school? What's his name?"

"David?" Cody asked.

"Yeah. I faked left, and he committed. So I slashed to the right and finger-rolled it in. It was awesome! I would have gotten the bucket and gone to the line."

Cody, feeling self-conscious about wearing his brother's shoes, pulled his feet back under the bleachers.

"I didn't even know you played basketball," Larry continued to blab. "Do you have a backboard over at your house?"

"It's out at the ranch." Cody waved his arms as he talked. "On the barn." Denver's black sleeveless T-shirt felt way too big on him. "Me and my brother usually shoot baskets during our lunch break."

"You've got to come over to my house, and we'll shoot some hoops. Did you see that backboard me and Dad put up? Primo, isn't it? Look at this . . . can you palm a ball left-handed?"

"I've hardly had a ball in my hand since last winter. Basketball isn't exactly my best sport," Cody admitted.

"Oh, yeah? What's your best sport?"

"Calf-roping."

"What?"

"You know, in the rodeo. When they rope and tie the calf."

"You're kidding. You do that?" Larry stopped dribbling to stare at Cody.

"Yeah, it's kind of a family thing. My oldest brother, Prescott, is on the Professional Rodeo Cowboy's Association tour."

"But that's not really a sport."

"Well, don't say that around my dad or brothers. You'll end up in the stock tank." Cody grinned. "How about you, Larry? What other sports do you play?"

He laughed. "Other sports? There isn't any other sport but basketball, is there? I play basketball every day of the year. You don't think I got this good sitting around playing Nintendo, do you?"

"Every day? Even when the weather's lousy?"

"When your dad's the high school coach, you can always get into the gym."

"Was he a coach back in Ohio?"

"Indiana! We're from Indiana."

"Same thing." Cody shrugged. "Does—"

A low, deep voice boomed, "Lewis, Larry!"

"Hey, it's my turn. Any college scouts in the audience?"

"There's no one in the audience," Cody informed him.

"Just teasing. Relax, dude. You're too uptight."

When Larry left, Cody stretched his legs back out in front of him.

My feet are too big. That's why I'm so awkward. Lord, are You sure You didn't make some mistakes here?

The tryouts were simple. Each guy shot two from the arc, two from the free-throw line, two jump shots, and two lay-ins from each side.

Then they ran laps.

Dribbled the length of the court twice.

Passed the ball twice to the coach.

Finally, took their best shots.

No offense.

No defense.

No jumping.

No rebounds.

Cody and nearly four dozen other kids watched as Larry went out into the center of the gym floor. He dribbled left, then right, crossed over behind him, between his legs, and then stopped at the three-point line and fired a shot to the basket. It slammed off the backboard and dropped through the net.

Cody shook his head. *I wonder if he was trying to bank it?*

Then he shot another that slammed into the front rim and bounced straight back at him. At the free-throw line, he swished the first and bricked the second. Both jump shots dropped into the net with precision—as did the lay-ins.

Larry is pretty good, even if he's not quite as good as he thinks.

When it was Cody's turn, he dribbled slowly to the three-point line.

"Hey, Clark, nice shoes!" someone hollered out. It sounded like J. J. Melton, but Cody was determined not to turn around.

The first shot slammed off the front rim, and he had to dive to catch the rebound, or it would have bounced to the other end of the gym. The second three-point attempt smacked into the glass and bounced into the net.

Yeah . . . I meant to do that.

Both free throws bounced on the rim and fell in, but he didn't make either jump shot. The lay-ins were a piece of cake. He even used his left hand when he drove on the left side. After he grabbed his rebound and turned to toss the ball to the coach, Cody noticed that Mr. Lewis was busy in a rather heated discussion with a lady with long, straight dark hair hanging to her waist.

He didn't even watch me! I did all that, and he wasn't even looking!

Cody jogged over to the stands and sat down next to Larry Lewis.

"Hey, I can help you with those jump shots," Larry insisted. "You're releasing the ball too soon. You've got to wait until you're at the top of your jump and then—"

"All right, Townie!" Cody hollered to his friend with jet-black hair worn in a butch haircut. "Nothin' but net!" He watched Jeremiah Yellowboy sink two "threes," two from the free-throw line, and then struggle a little with the jump shots and the lay-ins.

Cody turned to Larry. "He's strictly an outside shooter, you know."

"I could help him with his jump shots," Larry began, "if he would just . . . ."

A shrill whistle masked his final words.

"All right, everyone, listen up! I want you all out here at center court," Coach Lewis hollered. "Just sit on the floor in a circle around here. I've got a few announcements, and then I'll tell you which team you're on."

"He already has us on a team?" Jeremiah mumbled to Cody as they moved out to the middle of the polished wood floor.

"I guess so." Cody shrugged. "Maybe he decided before we got here."

With nearly fifty boys age twelve to fourteen huddled around him, Coach Lewis stood tall in the Indiana Pacers shorts and white T-shirt. His legs were as tan as his arms and face.

Jeremiah tossed him the leather basketball.

Coach Lewis, clipboard still in his left hand, turned to the basket at the east end of the gym and tossed the ball one-handed from the half-court line.

Cody stared in amazement. The ball hit nothing but net and dropped to the floor beneath the basket. He glanced over at Jeremiah, his mouth wide open.

"He does that all the time," Larry whispered. "It's no big deal really."

"Now you all know that I'm new here," the coach announced. "And some of you have been used to a different summer program. But once you get into the swing of things, I think you'll have a lot of fun this summer and improve your skills. That's what this three-on-three league is all about, right?

"I'll have a game schedule printed by Friday. We'll have open gym on Monday and Wednesday, but with all the other leagues, you'll have to find your own place to practice. I'm putting four players on most teams so you can bring in a sub if you need a breather. The two teams with the best records at the end of the season will be in a championship game. I've tried to keep you on a team with your friends if you requested that on your registration form.

"When I read your name, I want your team to move over and sit with each other on the stands. You'll need to stay together until I come around. Choose a team captain.

He'll be in charge of calling the others about practice and games. You'll need to decide your team name, too. No one can be the Huskies, so don't ask. Okay, as soon as I read your name, head to the stands."

He glanced over at the bleachers. Cody followed the coach's eyes to the lady with the long hair. Sitting next to her was a very thin girl wearing cut-off jeans, canvas basketball shoes, and a tie-dyed T-shirt.

"Eh . . ." The coach cleared his throat. "Guys, listen up. We will have something a little different. We have a young lady who will be playing in our league this year."

"The girls have their own league!" one kid called out.

"Yes, well . . . it has been pointed out to me that there is nothing in the rules that excludes a girl from this league, and until I check it out more thoroughly, Miss Hobbs will be—"

"My daughter's name is Feather Trailer-Hobbs," the lady corrected in a loud voice that would have made her a good cafeteria monitor.

"Feather?" Cody mumbled as he peered at Jeremiah.

"Don't stare at me—she's definitely not a tribal member," his dark-skinned friend replied with a straight-toothed grin.

The coach continued, "Here are the teams. Remember, choose a captain and a name."

Cody sprawled on the cool, hard floor, leaning his weight back on his hands. One by one he saw most of his friends assigned to other teams.

"I hope I get on a team with only three players," Larry

mumbled. "I don't like to have someone sub for me. Know what I mean?"

Cody nodded and watched another foursome jump up and scurry to the stands.

He leaned over to Jeremiah and held his hand over his mouth. "Hey, maybe it's you and me, partner."

"Only six more of us . . . and her." Jeremiah nodded to the stands where Miss Trailer-Hobbs sat.

The next to the last team was selected, and only Larry, Jeremiah, and Cody were left sitting on the floor.

"Well, fellas," Coach Lewis said pointing, "obviously you four are team number twelve."

"Four? There's only three of us here, Dad," Larry corrected.

"Miss Hobbs!" the coach called out.

"Trailer-Hobbs!" her mother corrected again.

"Yeah, eh, Feather, you're on team number twelve. Boys, introduce yourself to Feather and then select a captain and a team name."

"You've got to be kidding!" Larry protested. "Dad, wait, this definitely isn't going to work. You can't do this to me! I need to be on a team that—"

"You need some respect," Coach Lewis barked. "Give me six laps, or you're out the door!"

"Whoa!" Jeremiah gasped. "That's his own kid!"

They strolled over to an empty place in the bleachers as Larry ran laps. Cody whiffed a strange odor and glanced back. Feather Trailer-Hobbs followed them. He plopped down on a bench, as did the other two. She looked even taller and thinner up close.

"Hi, I'm Cody," he offered.

"I'm Feather." He tried not to stare at the double-pierced ears and the two sets of earrings on each ear.

"Eh . . . this is Jeremiah, but we call him Townie."

She squinted her eyes at Jeremiah. "Townie?"

"Yeah, 'Down-Town' Jeremiah Yellowboy. He can sink a three-pointer from anywhere in the building."

"Really?"

"Actually, only Cody calls me Townie. You can call me Jeremiah." A slight blush reflected through his round brown face.

"Are you Nez Perce?" she asked.

"Yeah. . . . My great, great-grandfather was Ollicut, Chief Joseph's brother."

"Wow, that's cool. Do you live in a tepee?"

Jeremiah looked at Cody, then back at Feather. "A tepee? Are you trying to be funny or what? I live in that blue house across the street."

"Hey, I wasn't putting you down," Feather explained. "I live in a tepee myself!"

"You do? Why?" Jeremiah asked.

"We just moved from Oregon and haven't had time to build a log house. We like the tepee so well we might use it all winter. How cold does it get in the winter?"

"Twenty below," Jeremiah offered.

"No, really," she insisted.

"Townie's right. It gets twenty below. Where do you live anyway? I don't remember any tepee around here."

"Out in the woods southwest of town."

"What grade are you in?" Jeremiah asked.

"I'm home-schooling, but I'm thirteen if that's what you wanted to know." She flipped the long, thin brown hair over her back and continued to smack her chewing gum.

"What I wanted to know is how come you didn't want to play in the girls' league?" Jeremiah asked.

"'Cause the girls are all wimps," she exploded. "They won't dive for the ball because they're afraid it will mess up their hair. Have you got a problem with that?"

Jeremiah swallowed hard. "Eh . . . nope. Maybe we should select a captain. I think Cody should be captain."

"I don't care." Feather tugged at the bright pink collar of her T-shirt. "But you can't call me. We don't have a telephone."

"You don't?"

"We aren't about to turn over the fruit of our labor to environment-depleting multinational corporations."

"Huh?" Jeremiah mumbled.

"You two are aware of the danger to our ecosystem, I hope." She glanced over to where her mother still sat in the stands. "We don't have any electricity for the same reason."

"You're kidding us!" Jeremiah gasped.

"Of course not. I thought *you*, of all the guys here, would understand."

"Me?" Jeremiah choked. "My people joined the twentieth century decades ago."

"Well," she huffed, "Cody can be captain."

"We better wait for Larry," Cody suggested.

"Is that his name?" Feather pointed toward the exhausted runner.

"Yeah, he's Larry Lewis, the coach's son."

"I watched him try out. You know, I could help him with his dribble. When I was younger, I used to dribble like that."

"Eh, don't tell him that." Cody raised his eyebrow and glanced over at Jeremiah. "So what's our team name going to be?"

"How about the Deadheads?" Feather suggested.

"The what?" Cody croaked.

"Then we could all wear tie-dyed shirts. I could dye them for us," Feather proposed.

"Maybe, you know . . . we should have something more traditional. How about the Bobcats?" Cody suggested.

Feather clutched her arms tight. "I absolutely refuse to be a part of a team that exploits innocent animals."

Jeremiah leaned back on the hard wooden bench. "Well, that leaves out my suggestion. I was thinking of calling us the Appaloosas. You have another suggestion, Clark?"

"Clark?" Feather repeated. "I thought your name was Cody?"

"Cody Clark."

Feather Trailer-Hobbs burst out laughing.

"My name's that funny?"

"No . . . no . . ." She giggled. "Don't you see? I'm on a team with Lewis and Clark! That makes me Sacajawea, doesn't it?"

"The Lewis and Clark Team! I like that," Jeremiah announced.

Cody rolled his eyes to the ceiling. "How about the Lewis and Clark Squad?"

Jeremiah Yellowboy hollered his approval.

That's when Larry Lewis trotted up to them out of breath.

"Hey, this is Feather. You know Townie, don't you?" Cody asked.

"Hi . . . I'm Larry. Listen up, guys," he panted. "I thought of what our team ought to be called while I was running laps."

"What?" Feather asked.

"The Hoosiers."

"What's a Hoosier?" Jeremiah pressed.

"Come on, everyone's heard of the Indiana Hoosiers!"

"What he asked was, 'What's a Hoosier?'" Feather insisted.

"People in Indiana are called Hoosiers."

"Why? What does it mean?" she asked.

"It means . . . well . . . It's not important what it means!" he fumed.

"We've decided to call the team the Lewis and Clark Squad," Jeremiah Yellowboy announced. "What do you think?"

Larry shrugged. "Lewis and Clark . . . just like the explorers?"

"Yeah, and I get to be Sacajawea!"

"She was a Shoshone. You don't have the right tan," Jeremiah kidded.

Feather laughed and wrinkled her nose. Cody noticed a wave of freckles wiggle when she did.

"Well, I've played three-on-three ball since I was born, so I suppose you want me to be captain," Larry suggested.

"Aye, aye, Captain Lewis." Feather faked a salute.

"That's fine with me," Cody added. "I've got to work most days and wouldn't have time to go out to Feather's with a message about practice."

"I can just phone her," Larry replied.

Jeremiah shook his head. "She doesn't have a phone."

"Doesn't have a phone? Why not?" Larry quizzed.

"Don't ask." Jeremiah made a face.

Cody stood and dribbled his basketball. "Feather, what position do you like to play? I mean, what's your strength? Have you played on a team before?"

"I like to play defense," she announced.

Larry Lewis stole the ball from Cody and began a series of dribbles behind his back and between his legs, circling Feather. "What do you mean, defense?"

Standing a good three inches taller than Larry, Feather doubled up and darted in front and stole the ball.

"That's what I mean. I like to steal the ball. Especially from egotistical boys!" She giggled.

Two

❖

*T*he license plates of the old dark blue Chevy pickup read Wyoming 4949. The broken right window had been replaced by a piece of cardboard that read: "Wal-Mart, We Sell for—." The bed of the truck was littered with used orange-colored baling string, several crushed Mountain Dew cans, and a couple of flakes of very old half-molded alfalfa hay.

From midway on the door on down, a layer of baked, thick, dry mud made it impossible to even see the paint. The left taillight was nothing more than clear plastic red tape that had been hurriedly applied. Inside the cab, Cody spotted a McDonald's paper sack that looked like it had been used as a grease rag, one leather glove, an ice scraper, two cassette tapes without cases, and something on the dash that looked as if it had at one time been a piece of pizza.

The radio antenna had been snapped off about two inches above the hood, and a piece of coat hanger now took its place. Three of the tires were Goodyears, but the fourth was a highly worn Bridgestone.

All in all, it didn't look a lot different from many early 1950s pickups Cody had seen in and around his hometown of Halt, Idaho. What surprised him was that it was parked out in the middle of Eureka Blaine's horse pasture.

And it had been there for three days.

A column of dust rose from near the blacktopped road almost two miles away, and Cody knew it was Denver's Dodge pickup. He finished dumping the alfalfa pellets into the feed trough, jogged back up the dirt drive to the gravel road, and then sprinted over to the big, faded red barn.

Cowboy boots are lousy for running, but if I can catch Denver, maybe he'll give me a ride back to town, and I won't have to ride my bike.

Cody's seventeen-year-old brother sped into the ranch and parked by the corrals. Even before the dust cleared, shouts came from the back of the truck.

"Hey, cowboy, how about a basketball game?" Jeremiah hollered. He was wearing a red and black Chicago Bulls tank top.

Cody trotted over to the back of the rig. "What are you guys doing here?" he asked Larry. "I thought we were going to practice at your house."

"I broke the rim on a reverse slam," Larry announced, his straight blond hair hanging down to his eyes.

"You did what?"

"He had the basket set at seven feet," Feather explained as all three piled out of the back of the pickup. She wore her cut-off jeans and a mostly bright yellow tie-dyed T-shirt. Her long brown hair was pulled back in a ponytail that stretched halfway down her back.

"Yeah, well . . . it was a reverse slam," Larry boasted. "Anyway, you'd think a brand-new rim would be bolted on better than that."

"Denver was just leaving the house to go to Lewiston and said he'd give us a lift out here." Jeremiah Yellowboy dribbled across the dirt yard and fired a long shot at the basket that hung from a backboard nailed to the barn wall.

Nothing but net.

Cody waved at his brother as Denver roared out of the yard and back toward the paved county road.

"This is where you practice?" Larry scowled. "How in the world do you dribble on this dirt and . . . "

"Cow manure," Feather put in as she dragged her canvas basketball shoes across the soil. "It's mainly dried cow manure."

"Hey, it's not bad now," Cody explained. "You ought to see it when it's wet and muddy in the spring."

"Gross!" Lewis protested. "That is totally gross, Clark."

The three of them moseyed over to where Jeremiah continued to shoot baskets.

"Does Denver have a girlfriend?" Feather asked.

The three boys stared at her.

Feather likes Denver? Help me not to laugh, Lord.

"Hey, girls mature faster than boys. Everyone knows that!" she defended herself.

Cody shrugged. "Well . . . he's going out with Becky Haley. You know—the cheerleader?"

"The head cheerleader at Halt High!" Jeremiah added

as he plucked the ball out of Cody's hand and dribbled it twice. Feather stole it, then chucked a hard pass to Larry, who staggered back in surprise. He recovered enough to fire up a twelve-foot jump shot.

Nothing but net.

"He just happens to be my type!" she pouted.

Well, Feather girl, you aren't his type. Denver likes the more . . . more mature type.

"Did you guys bring out my basketball shoes?" Cody asked as all four jogged toward the ball.

"Shoes? What a wimp!" Jeremiah teased.

"I can't practice with my cowboy boots on!" he protested.

"Why not?" Larry chided as he drove for a lay-in. "You can play over there where the manure's deep!"

"Really, guys, come on. One of you brought my shoes, right?"

"Forget it, Clark. This is wilderness basketball. In fact, I'm really glad I'm not wearing one of my good pairs," Larry announced. "Hey, don't worry about it; we'll stick you under the basket or something. Anyway, I have our practice schedule all figured out."

"Practice schedule?" Jeremiah dribbled the ball out to the edge of the barn. "I thought we'd just play some two-on-two." His shot bounced off the front rim. Cody pulled down the rebound over the outstretched arms of Larry Lewis and buzzed the ball back out to Jeremiah. He tossed up another shot.

Nothing but net.

"Look, we need to get going on this practice schedule," Larry insisted.

"Aye, aye, Captain Lewis!" Feather joked.

"Have you really got a practice schedule for us?" Jeremiah asked.

"Yep. I stayed up pretty late last night writing it out. I thought we'd begin with a couple of ball-handling exercises."

"I don't need to practice that," Feather protested.

"Look, we are all going to practice everything," Larry insisted.

And they did.

The Clark ranch sat on 3,200 acres located four miles north of Halt, right where the pine trees lap out onto the edge of the sprawling, rolling Camas Prairie of north-central Idaho. To the west, pines, firs, cedars, spruce, and tamaracks crowded the canyons and coulees. The eastern horizon was mostly hay fields, which were turning slightly brown in the mid-June summer sun.

There was no shade on the east end of the Clark barn, and after ninety minutes of continuous practice, Larry Lewis found his team bolting toward the corrals.

"Hey, where you guys going?" he hollered.

"Time for a break, Larry," Cody called back.

"You can keep on if you want to," Jeremiah added.

Feather skipped ahead of them. "We need a drink. Cody said the best water's over there."

Cody led the quartet across the gravel road, up Eureka Blaine's driveway, and into his shady backyard.

"We're going to drink out of the stock tank?" Larry complained. His basketball shoes, socks, and legs were covered with a fine red dust.

"Not the stock tank. Just the faucet that supplies the stock tank. It's the coldest, sweetest water north of town."

It took several moments for each one to get sufficiently filled. The yard was mostly packed dirt, with a clump of cottonwood trees supplying the shade. Next to the trees were several worn chairs, wooden crates, and an old car seat. All four found a place to collapse. Larry lay down on the car seat and tossed the basketball straight above him, catching it and throwing it back up.

"You take care of this place, do you?" Feather asked.

"I just feed the animals, that's all," Cody explained. "Mr. Blaine's a horse trainer and trader. He's got this 160-acre homestead. It's all pasture, except for the hay barn, the corrals, and Eureka's old single-wide trailer house. Most of the summer months, he travels to rodeos in Idaho and the northwest supplying horses for steer wrestlers, hazers, and ropers. My brothers have all taken turns looking after his animals. Now it's my turn."

Jeremiah rocked his chair back against a tree. "You get paid for it?"

"Sort of." Cody pulled off his lace-up roper boots and rubbed his raw feet.

Feather wandered over toward the old trailer. "What do you mean, sort of?" she called back.

"Every day that I feed I get four dollars on my account," Cody explained.

"What do you mean, your account?" she asked.

"When my account reaches $800, Eureka will give me a good roping horse."

"That would take 200 days!" Feather exclaimed, peeking into one of the trailer windows. "How many summers will that take you?"

"About three." Cody shrugged. "But Eureka has some of the best roping horses in the state."

"Hey, that's cool. Then when you get the horse, you can sell him and make a nice profit, right?" Larry asked.

"Why would I want to do that?"

"Oh, yeah . . . Cowboy Cody. Hey, that's kind of cool—Cowboy Cody. Maybe I'll just call you that from now on."

"And we'll call you Hoosier-head Lewis," Jeremiah countered.

Cody glanced at Feather. She was shielding her eyes and staring in the window by the back door. "What are you doing?"

"Just looking at this trailer. It's big inside."

"Big?" Jeremiah questioned. "It's only ten feet wide."

"Well, it's bigger than our tepee," she replied strolling back to the others. "Hey, how'd this guy get a name like Eureka?"

"It means 'I've found it,' or something like that. I guess when his grandfather moved up here to homestead, he called this place Eureka," Cody explained.

"How about your name?" Feather asked him. She rubbed her nose with the back of her hand, and her freckles all waved. "Were you named after Buffalo Bill Cody?"

"Sort of, I guess. I was named after Cody, Wyoming, and it was named after Buffalo Bill."

"Why Cody, Wyoming?" she prodded.

"All of us are named after rodeo towns. Dad used to go down the road, and Mom was a barrel racer. So my oldest brother is named after Prescott, Arizona, and my second brother after Reno, Nevada—"

"And Denver got his name from Denver, Colorado," Feather finished for him.

"There's a rodeo in Weippe," Jeremiah laughed. "Good thing your folks didn't have more kids."

"Speaking of names—how did you get the name Feather?" Cody asked.

"My mother said it was a very spiritual experience," she reported, tilting her head slightly in the air.

"Oh? You mean they prayed about it, and the Lord told them what to call you?" Cody quizzed.

"Not that kind of spiritual. Actually, the trees named me."

"What?" Cody's mouth dropped open as he glanced at the other two boys and then back at Feather.

She strutted around the dirt yard as she spoke. "See, right before I was born, my mom was lying out in the forest and—"

"She was what?" Larry asked.

"She likes to lie out in the forest on her back and stare up at the trees and meditate. Is that all right with you?" she barked.

"Yeah . . . sure . . . whatever," Larry stammered.

"Anyway, as I was saying, she was looking up at the sky, trying to figure out what to call me. Then all of a sudden it came to her."

"A voice?" Jeremiah asked.

"No! A feather floated down out of the trees, and that's when she decided to call me Feather. She thinks of it as the trees providing her a name." She turned to Jeremiah. "Don't your people name their kids like that?"

"Me? I was named after Jeremiah in the Bible. All of us were named after people in the Bible."

"How about Two Ponies and Sweetwater?" Cody asked.

"Those are their tribal names. Mom named them Joel and Micah, but the tribal elders give you a name about the time you get to be a teenager. Some like to go by their tribal names. Some still use their birth names."

"How big a family do you have?" Feather asked.

"Two older brothers and four younger sisters."

Feather stopped pacing to study Jeremiah Yellowboy. His brown legs were covered with red dust just like the others. "That's a large family."

"You're telling me. We all live in a three-bedroom house, too."

"But," Feather pursued grinning, "you didn't tell me the most important part. How did you get a last name like Yellowboy?"

"That's easy. Have you ever seen a '66 Winchester rifle?"

"A gun?" Feather held up her hand in protest. "We don't believe in guns. They mark the ending of civilization and the beginning of building a society of social psychopaths."

"Huh?" Cody, Larry, and Jeremiah choked in unison.

"Well," Jeremiah cleared his throat, "the old 1866

Winchesters had a brass receiver, and they shine real yellow in the sunlight . . . so everyone started calling them yellowboys. When my great-grandfather decided we needed a last name, he took that one because he liked the way it sounded."

"Hey, are you guys ready to go back and practice some more?" Larry challenged.

"Don't you think of anything but basketball?" Jeremiah chided.

"What else is there? Come on, we'll shoot for teams. Let's play to twenty by twos and threes, losers out. We'll have to call our own fouls."

All four hiked out of the yard and along the corral fence. Jeremiah climbed to the top rail and pointed out into the pasture. "Hey, how come Mr. Blaine parks that old truck out there?"

Cody climbed up next to him. "You guys want to hear a mystery?"

"Yeah." Feather mounted the top rail and towered above the boys.

"Are we going to practice or not?" Larry insisted.

"You see that truck? Well, it doesn't belong to Mr. Blaine. In fact, it just showed up in that pasture three days ago. I don't have any idea how it got there, why it's there, or who it belongs to."

"Oh, yeah?" Jeremiah shaded his eyes for a closer look.

"The first day I saw it out here, I figured some old rodeo friend had stopped by and spent the night at Eureka's. Denver said that happens sometimes. Yesterday I peeked in the trailer windows but couldn't see anyone. Now I'm beginning to think the truck has been abandoned or something. Maybe I should call the sheriff. What do you guys think?"

"I think . . . ," Jeremiah began, "that someone stole the truck, drove it until it ran out of gas, and just abandoned it in the field, and hitchhiked to town."

"It was nice of them to close the gate behind them." Cody pointed to the barbed-wire gate.

"Listen, I know what it is," Feather broke in. "There was this drug deal that went bad, and—"

"A drug deal in Halt, Idaho?" Cody scoffed.

"Eh . . . well, he's from out of state, Wyoming, right? So he's being chased, and he gets shot, and he races down this road trying to escape those who are after him. So he pulls in here and . . . and closes the gate so they would think it just belonged out here in the pasture."

"Then what happened?" Jeremiah's dark brown eyes grew large.

"Well . . . he ran down into the woods to hide, and . . ."

"And what?" Jeremiah prodded.

Feather raised her eyebrows. "He died."

"He died!" Jeremiah gasped.

"Yep. That's my theory. If we were to comb the woods down on the other side of that creek, we'd find a bloated body lacerated with gunshot wounds and—"

"Yuck!" Jeremiah groaned. "You are really, really gross!"

"Thank you," Feather said in triumph.

"What's your theory, Larry?" Cody asked.

"I think it was driven in here by a spy."

"Hey, that's cool." Jeremiah nodded approvingly.

"Yes, and it's just a clever camouflage of a high-powered camera and microphone obviously operated by remote control."

"Maybe it belongs to James Bond!" Jeremiah laughed.

"No. The highly computerized equipment is at this very moment pointed over at Cody's barn."

"My barn? Why is it pointed over there?"

"Because it's operated by a spy from the Youth Three-on-Three Summer Basketball League who is determined to find out our secret plans."

"Basketball? We should have known this would lead back to basketball!" Feather groaned as she climbed down into the corral.

"Well, basketball is my middle name."

"Is that what the B. stands for?" Cody asked.

"No, the B. stands for Bird," Larry explained.

"You mean your middle name is Bird?" Jeremiah pressed.

Cody glanced at the slightly shorter blond. "Larry Bird Lewis?"

"Yeah, my little brother is Kevin McHale Lewis, and I'm Larry Bird Lewis, named after the greatest basketball player ever."

"You might get a debate over that," Cody laughed. "Hey, where are you going?" he hollered at Feather as she cut across the pasture.

"I'm going to look at the registration on that truck."

Cody hopped down and followed her. "We can't do that. That's not our truck. We can't rummage around inside it!"

"I'm only going to look at the registration," she insisted. "When you find a lost wallet in the street, you look to see who to return it to, don't you? Well, I'm going to see who we should return it to."

Cody grabbed Feather's arm. It felt even skinnier than it looked. "What if someone catches us going through their pickup?"

"Who's going to catch us? You said no one's been around here for days."

"Yeah, but . . ."

"Stay there on the fence if you're too chicken," Feather challenged. She pulled her arm away and ran toward the truck.

All three boys raced after her, Larry in the lead.

"It's locked!" she called out. "Try the other door."

"It's locked, too," Jeremiah reported.

Feather shoved open a wind wing on the truck and snaked her left hand into the cab and along the window ledge.

"What are you doing?" Cody hollered.

"I'm unlocking the door. What does it look like?"

"But you can't—"

"I just did." She pulled her arm out and flipped her long brown ponytail back over her shoulders. Then she yanked open the door and slid across the partly ripped seat cover. "Where's the registration?"

Jeremiah stuck his head through the doorway. "Maybe it's in that thing on the sun visor."

"It's covered with dust."

"Look in there anyway," Larry suggested.

Lord, I sure hope no one gets mad at us for looking in this truck. I knew I should have told the sheriff.

"Yeah, there's some papers in here," she reported. "This looks like car insurance and this . . ."

"What is it?" Cody pressed.

"The registration."

"What does it say?" Jeremiah crowded closer and tried to look over her shoulder.

"Guess who owns this truck?" she said as she clutched the paper to her chest.

"Larry Bird?" Cody teased.

"Funny," Larry sniped, "very funny!"

"I know, I know!" Jeremiah laughed. "It's the original truck Lewis and Clark used!"

Larry was almost hysterical. "I thought they drove a Ford!"

"Clowns. All boys are clowns!" Feather was piqued. "Come on, guys, guess."

"I know." Cody poked Jeremiah in the ribs. "It belonged to Jesse James! Didn't he drive a Ford? No, no, he was killed by a Ford!"

Jeremiah was laughing so hard tears rolled out the corners of his eyes.

"Jesse James was run over by a Ford?" Larry hooted.

"No, he was shot by a Ford. Robert Ford."

"Knock it off, you guys, or I won't tell you who owns this truck!" Feather huffed.

"I think it was some Mafia godfather who staggered down into the trees and died," Jeremiah proposed.

"Maybe we should go look for his bloated, lacerated

body!" Larry's comment got all three boys rolling with laughter.

Feather shoved the paper back above the sun visor, climbed out of the truck, locked the door, and slammed it shut.

"Wait! We didn't see the registration," Cody complained.

"I did," she announced as she flipped the basketball out of Larry's hands and raced toward the corral fence.

Three

*That ties it up—seventeen all!" Larry shouted, his bright blue eyes flashing.

Cody's black sleeveless ProRodeo T-shirt stuck to the sweat on his back. "You only have fifteen," he corrected.

"What? No! Jeremiah's three-pointer made it fifteen. Then I just made that incredible turn-around, faded-away jumper to tie it up." Larry's voice sounded wound up and tight.

"Townie's bank shot only made it thirteen!" Cody insisted.

"Oh, come on, just because we tied you up . . ." Then Larry turned for help, waving his long, thin arms and big hands. "Jeremiah?"

"I, eh, I forget what we had." Yellowboy wore a green Sonics tank top. "We either have fifteen or seventeen, that's for sure."

Only Larry's knees shone between the baggy nylon shorts and the over-the-calf white socks. "We have seventeen!" he shouted.

Lord, I don't know why Larry has to win every time. This takes all the fun out of practice.

"Look, you have fifteen," Feather chided, "but if it will make you feel better, we can all pretend you have seventeen."

"Pretend! You've got to be kidding." Larry's face flushed red in the bright Idaho sun.

"Let's play basketball," Jeremiah insisted.

"We can't play until we have the score right," Larry pouted.

"Well, I can." Feather knocked the ball out of Larry's hand and quickly passed it over to Cody. "Bring it in, partner. Let's finish them off right now." Her T-shirt was splashed with greens, oranges, and yellows.

Cody checked the ball by bouncing it to Jeremiah Yellowboy, who tossed it back to him. "All right, Feather girl, it's victory time!" he boasted.

Larry waved his hands in protest. "Wait . . . we can't play if we don't know the score!"

"You guard Feather. I've got the cowboy," Jeremiah hollered. "You're goin' down, paleface. I've got on my war paint. Prepare to meet the pride of the Nez Perce Nation!"

"Time out!" Larry screamed, forming a T with his hands.

Cody dribbled toward the right side of the barn, then turned, and fired a quick pass back to Feather, which was partially deflected by Jeremiah. The ball took a wild bounce off the dirt, and Larry stole it. He drove toward the left side of the basket. Feather sprinted after him, her long brown hair flying behind her. Just as Larry started to lift the ball off the dribble, she whisked in, grabbed the ball, and quickly passed it to Cody.

"Foul! That was a foul!" Larry hollered.

"Foul? I didn't touch you!" Feather protested.

"You hit me right here!" Larry pointed to the back of his left arm.

"Where's the bruise?" she demanded.

He brushed his blond hair out of his eyes. "Well, you didn't bruise me."

She folded her long arms and glared down at Larry. "I can if you'd like me to!"

"Come on, you two," Cody coaxed. He bounced the ball over to Lewis. "We call our own fouls, and you called it. So bring it in."

"What do you mean, bring it in? I was shooting. I go to the line. It's one-on-one."

"Shooting? You were still dribbling, and it was a clean steal, and you know it!" Feather hollered, her grayish green eyes narrowed.

"Come on, Larry, you weren't shooting," Jeremiah coached. "Check the ball. Let's bring it in."

"I deserve to go to the line." Larry Lewis marched to the free-throw line, a faded mark in the dirt drawn earlier in the day by the toe of Cody's basketball shoe.

"Are you serious?" Jeremiah pressed.

"Get up there for a rebound," Larry ordered. "Not that I'm going to miss either shot."

And he didn't.

"All right! Nineteen to seventeen! One more point and we win, Jeremiah."

"Yeah, whatever," Cody mumbled. *What's the point in winning if you have to cheat to do it?* He took the ball and had Larry check it back to him. He flung the ball to Feather and darted to the right side of the basket. Jeremiah kept between him and the basket. Feather's pass to Cody was hard and high, but he pulled it down right against the barn wall and faked going to the basket. Jeremiah left his feet to try and block the shot, and Larry ran over to double-team him. Just before both boys crashed into him, Cody bounce-passed the ball back out to Feather, who was standing alone at the nearly obliter-ated three-point line.

Larry crawled across the dirt trying to get to his feet. "No!" he screamed.

"Shoot it!" Cody yelled.

She did.

Cody and Jeremiah were still sitting in the dirt when the ball descended toward the faded orange hoop.

Nothing but net.

"She wasn't behind the three-point line," Larry cried. "That was only two! It's tied. Next bucket wins!"

"Larry, my man, we just got beat," Jeremiah stated. "Feather's still standing behind the line."

She stuck out her tongue at Larry Lewis while he sulked over to retrieve the basketball from the dirt.

"Well . . . just barely. It was twenty to nineteen, right?"

"Whatever." Cody shrugged. "This is only practice, Larry. We're all on the same team. Why make it such a big deal?"

"Yeah, we're just practicing," Feather added.

"My dad says if you want to be a winner, you have to practice winning!" Larry insisted. "You guys couldn't beat us in the gym. There's just too much luck out here at the ranch."

"When's your dad going to get your rim fixed?" Cody asked. "At least you have some concrete we could dribble on if we practiced over there."

"Well, I sort of . . . I mean, Dad said since I broke it, I'll have to pay for it."

"What will it cost?" Feather asked.

"Twenty-five bucks."

Feather led the quartet as they hiked across the road to Eureka Blaine's. "Do you have the money?"

"Eh . . . no, not really."

"I thought you said you had a Michael Jordan die-cut basketball card worth thirty-five dollars? You could sell it and . . ." Cody's size twelve basketball shoes slapped a fog of fine dust about his feet.

"Are you kidding? Sell that card? Ten years from now it will be worth a couple hundred. I'm not selling it."

"So we keep practicing at the ranch," Feather concluded. "It's okay. I kind of like it out here. I mean, the sky's clear, the sun's warm, the breeze is cool, and it's really quiet."

"Except for Larry's crying," Jeremiah teased.

"I wasn't crying! I was protesting."

"It's so peaceful," Feather continued, as she drank out of the freeze-proof faucet.

"Peaceful?" Jeremiah questioned as he waited in line for a drink. "You live out in the middle of the woods with your parents and no sisters and brothers—talk about peaceful. One of my brothers and his girlfriend got into a screaming argument in the living room about two in the morning and kept me awake half the night."

"What were they yelling about?" Cody asked.

Jeremiah glanced over at Feather and then back at Cody. "Oh, you know . . . nothin'. Adult stuff. Anyway, I was too sleepy to pay attention."

"Well, I don't always have it peaceful out at my place either. Sometimes my mother chants almost all night long," Feather reported.

"What kind of chants?" Larry raised his eyebrows and looked at the other two boys.

"She gets energized by getting her metabolism in sync with nature."

All three boys glanced around at the other two without moving their heads.

"But I don't want to talk about it." Feather twisted her long hair with her fingers. "Let's talk about that old truck. Did you tell your dad it belonged to somebody in California?"

"Eh . . . no," Cody admitted.

"Why? Just because I didn't let you guys see the registration yesterday? You don't believe me or what? I wasn't lying, you know."

"I believe you," Cody replied. "But if I told him what the registration said, he'd ask how I knew. Then I'd have to tell him we broke in and—"

"We didn't break in. We merely unlocked the door and peeked in a little, that's all."

"Well, my dad would call it breaking in. He sort of figures that the truck isn't doing any harm, so it's just none of our business."

"Let's go look at it again," Jeremiah suggested.

"Why? Nothing's changed since yesterday," Cody stalled.

Jeremiah stood up and strolled toward the pasture. "Maybe we can find some footprints to follow."

"And," Larry laughed, "maybe they lead down to the woods!"

Cody picked up on the sentence. "Where we're bound to discover—"

"Don't say it," Jeremiah joined in. "It's just too gruesome, bloated, and lacerated to think about."

"Are you enjoying making fun of me?" Feather broke in.

"Making fun of you? Of course not!" Cody assured her. "But we have to be honest. There in the forest we could find something too hideous even to be seen on sleaze TV."

"A frightening spectacle sure to cause nightmares for years to come," Jeremiah intoned.

Larry faked a gasp. "You don't mean there could be a . . . a . . ."

"Yes!" Cody shouted. "Right there in Eureka Blaine's woods there could be . . . a mutilated Taco Bell burrito!"

"Aahhhh!" Larry grabbed his throat and pretended to gag.

Jeremiah collapsed in a fake faint on a bale of hay.

"The ultimate gross-out!" Cody laughed.

"Are you three quite finished?" Feather sulked. "We

happen to be living in very violent and dangerous times. Murders do happen."

"When was the last one in Halt, Idaho?" Larry asked.

"1926," Cody replied.

"What happened then?" Feather asked.

"I read something about it once. This guy from Missouri tried robbing the Lewis County Bank. But something went wrong, and he ended up not getting any money. But he killed Hadley Sloburg, the teller." Cody climbed up on the corral fence and stared out at the silent pickup.

"Did they arrest him?" Larry asked.

"I don't know if they arrested him, but they hung him."

"What?" Larry choked. "No trial or anything?"

"Nope. And they wouldn't even bury him in the cemetery. Some rancher took the body home and buried it on his place. They said they didn't want some murderer sharing the dirt with their loved ones."

Feather climbed up alongside Cody. "What was his name?"

"The murderer?"

"Yeah."

"Seven Weslow."

"His name was Seven?" she probed.

"Yep. I guess his folks ran out of names after a while."

"So the lynch mob grabbed him and hung him?" Larry asked.

"That's frontier justice, Mr. Larry Lewis." Cody shrugged.

"But that was 1926. You can't call that frontier justice. The frontier was all gone by then, wasn't it?" Larry quizzed.

Cody glanced over at Jeremiah and then back at Larry. "Gone? We're livin' on the frontier right now, partner!"

"Now?" Larry's mouth dropped open. "You mean if someone killed a teller at the bank, people would still hang the guy?"

"There would be plenty who'd want to, that's for sure," Jeremiah conceded.

Larry climbed up on the corral rail next to the others. "What did you mean, this is still the frontier?"

"I mean, around here folks heat their homes with woodstoves, shoot wild game for food—not sport, think nothing about riding their horse down to the store, and figure criminals should get what they deserve and get it mighty quick."

"Yeah," Feather continued, "doesn't it sort of mean you have the freedom to do whatever you want as long as it's on your place and it doesn't bother anyone else?"

Cody continued, "People around here don't much trust outsiders, government programs, or people who aren't willing to work hard."

"Oh, well, that's not really . . . not like living on the old frontier," Larry objected.

"And they don't mention the secret Native American conspiracy either." Jeremiah Yellowboy grinned.

"The wh-what?" Larry stammered.

"Yeah, Townie and his people have a secret plan to take over all the three-point basketball shots for the entire town of Halt. Someday soon no one but tribal members will be allowed to shoot threes," Cody explained.

"Yeah," Jeremiah jumped in. "We don't figure we need to keep all the three-point shots to ourselves. So we'll probably sell licenses. So for like twenty-five dollars a year, you palefaces can shoot threes. There'll be a limit, of course . . . like two a day or no more than twenty in a year. Being members of the Nez Perce Nation, we could shoot 'em day and night, anytime, and on anyone's basket without limit."

"Real funny!" Larry mocked. "But I say Halt isn't much different from a small town in Indiana." All four were now sitting on the top rail of the fence staring across the pasture at the old pickup.

"Now that's where you're wrong, Larry, my man," Cody jibed. "In Indiana a town this size is small. On the Idaho frontier, it's a midsized city."

"Halt?" Larry chided. "The name itself is a small-town name. Where did it come from anyway?"

Cody looked over at Jeremiah. Both had wide grins.

"It's my turn to go first," Cody asserted.

"What do you mean, it's your turn?" Larry questioned.

"Never mind. See, here's the deal. . . . Back in the old days when there were no towns between Lewiston and Mt. Idaho, they put a toll road right up the side of Spotted Horse Canyon. Well, it was pretty steep and crooked, and I guess the stage drivers, passengers, and horses were pretty tired by the time they finally made it up here. They slowed down and let the horses just walk for a while. Well, pretty soon the highwaymen figured out this was a good place to rob the stage."

"You mean they really did stuff like that?"

Cody scowled at Larry, then continued. "Anyway, the

stagecoach robbers would always jump out in front of the rig and yell, 'Halt!' I guess that happened so often that when the railroad came through after the turn of the century and they opened a lumber mill, they just called the town Halt."

Larry studied Cody's face for a minute. Then he turned to Jeremiah Yellowboy. "Is any of that true?"

"Maybe," Jeremiah whooped.

"What's so funny?" Larry pressed. "You made that all up, didn't you?"

"I didn't make it up," Cody insisted.

"Well, is it true?"

"Maybe." Cody tried to stop laughing. "Come on, let's go check out my pickup." He jumped down from the rail and scurried toward the middle of the mixed grass pasture.

Feather hurried to stay up with him. "What do you mean, your pickup?"

"If nobody claims it, my dad said Eureka would probably let me have it."

"You? You're only thirteen. What are you going to do with a truck?"

"My dad sometimes lets me drive his truck on the ranch."

"But it's over two years before you can get a license."

"Well, it might be two years before we know who abandoned this rig," Cody countered.

All four hiked over to the truck. Jeremiah climbed into the back and sat down on the tailgate. A long-legged brown horse peeked over the barbed wire fence and watched their every move.

"Would you really want this old pickup?" Larry asked.

"I'd paint it a different color," Cody replied.

"A different color? What color is it now? It's all mud." Larry snickered.

"Hey, it's an earth-tone brown." Feather smiled in a way that made her freckles wiggle. "It's environmentally correct!"

"Correct? It's a dump! Look at this garbage." Jeremiah picked up a wide slice of old pizza from the pickup bed. "Whoa . . . this is cool. It's plastic or rubber or something."

"It's what?" Cody climbed up on the running board and looked at Jeremiah.

"It's a fake pizza." Jeremiah called out. "Look at this!"

"No wonder it looks so gross," Feather commented. "Did I ever tell you my mother doesn't like anything on her pizza but alfalfa sprouts and mushrooms?"

Cody stared through the glass of the front window into the cab. "Wait a minute!" he shouted. "It's gone!"

"What's gone?" Jeremiah walked to the front of the bed of the truck still carrying the rubber slice of pizza.

"Yesterday that piece of fake pizza was lying right up there on the dash!" Cody waved his arms when he talked, and his muscles revealed his summers spent loading bales of hay. "Now it's gone, and we find it in the back of the truck."

"I remember it being up there!" Feather confirmed.

Jeremiah flung the slice into the back of the truck. "You mean someone tossed it back here?"

"Then someone was out here at the truck!" Larry hollered.

Feather tried to open the door. "Someone unlocked the rig, got in, and then locked it back up again."

"And chucked the fake pizza back here!" Jeremiah pointed.

"Who?"

"When?"

"Why?"

"This is weird, really weird." Cody circled the pickup. "Someone came out here, sat in the truck, and then snuck off before being spotted? That doesn't make sense."

"Maybe it's a homeless man who sleeps in the truck at night," Larry suggested.

"Sure," Cody continued, "a homeless man who has a key to this truck."

"And likes to eat rubber pizza!" Jeremiah whooped.

"Don't be ridiculous," Feather insisted. "It seems obvious that this is a departure point for an alien space ship, which is right now hovering above our atmosphere. This teleport is merely disguised as a pickup in order not to attract attention. This might be a window into a parallel galaxy! Why, if I hadn't hopped out of the truck and locked it yesterday, right now we could all be standing on the planet Xeobolope, about to be turned into robotic slaves."

"Aliens! Why didn't we think of that? There might be aliens all around us!" Larry bantered.

"Spying on us from the woods!" Cody put in.

"Cleverly disguised as . . . as Taco Bell burrito wrappers!" Jeremiah shouted.

"I have noticed an increased number of burrito wrappers out alongside the highway," Larry pointed out.

Jeremiah swept his arm across the pasture. "That proves my theory. It's an invasion!"

"Very funny! You three have the combined imagination of a slug!" Feather sulked.

Cody stopped in front of the truck and looked carefully in the tall pasture grass.

"Well, this isn't imaginary. Somebody walked across the pasture in the last twelve hours or so. The timothy grass is still all mashed down."

"No kidding? Wow!" Jeremiah jumped down and scurried up next to Cody. "Where are the tracks leading?"

Cody stared at Larry . . . then at Jeremiah . . . then at Feather. "They're headed straight into the trees!"

Feather crossed her arms and tilted her head. "See! I told you to look in the woods!"

Four

✺

*T*he sound of a hay truck horn stopped all four before they wandered more than ten feet from the pickup.

"It's your brother Denver!" Feather called.

"What's he want? It isn't time for him to pick us up, is it?" Cody glanced at his wrist and then remembered he wasn't wearing a watch. He shielded his eyes and observed the position of the sun. "It's not noon yet," he pronounced.

They scampered over the corral fence and met Denver near Eureka Blaine's trailer house.

"What are you doing at Eureka's?" Denver asked from the open window of the dark green cab.

"We came over for a drink and were checking out that old pickup," Cody explained.

Feather scooted up in front of Cody. "Hi, Denver!"

"Feather girl," Denver called out, "did you teach these guys anything about basketball today?"

She smirked at Larry. "I taught one of them something."

"Is it time to go home already?" Cody asked.

"Larry's dad called. Your first game has been bumped

up to tonight. The Salmon River Rats had to reschedule, so he just switched them with you."

"Tonight?" Larry choked. "We can't play tonight! We aren't ready. We need more practice! He can't do that. How come we have to be the ones who change? It's not fair!"

Denver shrugged. "You can take that up with your dad. Mom said you'd better not run yourselves out this morning."

Feather pulled Jeremiah out of the way so that she could slide in next to Denver. All four crowded and squeezed their way into the cab of the big truck.

"Who are we scheduled to play tonight?" Cody asked.

"The Ponderosa Pirates," Denver reported.

"The Pirates! Our first game is against the Pirates?" Jeremiah gasped.

"Who's on the Pirates?" Larry asked.

"Oh, just Devin Scott, Rocky Hammers, and J. J. Melton!" Jeremiah groaned. "My forehead still hurts from that head butt last year."

"A head butt in basketball?"

"The Pirates are a very physical team. 'Course, Devin's about six-foot-two, and J. J. can bench-press 200 pounds."

"Oh, man. How about that other guy—Rocky?" Larry asked.

"Rocky's the one that put Townie on the bench last year," Cody reported.

"Yeah, but can they play basketball?" Larry quizzed. "Maybe we can outrun them."

"You'd better pray that we can outrun them," Jeremiah offered. "And I don't mean just during the game."

"No wonder the Salmon River Rats found something else to do," Feather scoffed.

"Hey, we're quick," Larry suggested. "We can run them down."

"Why?" Jeremiah asked.

"So we can win!"

Jeremiah glanced out the window of the speeding truck. "Why would we want to do that?"

Larry looked at Cody and then back at Jeremiah Yellowboy. "Are you telling me we should try to lose this game?"

"Nope. I'm saying we should try not to receive any life-threatening injuries."

"Oh, come on, they aren't that tough, are they?" he asked Cody.

"Devin will start on the high school varsity next year," Denver broke in.

"Yeah, and so will Rocky—if he doesn't get arrested or something," Jeremiah added.

"Are you going to come to our game tonight, Denver?" Feather asked.

"Nah, me and Becky are going to a movie. Maybe we can catch the next one."

Feather bit her lower lip and stared out the front window. She didn't say another word all the way back to town.

Cody spent most of the afternoon in his backyard roping a plastic steer head stuck into a bale of hay and thinking about the coming game.

Lord, it's not going to be very fun playing the Pirates. I don't know why they have to treat everyone so mean. I really don't mind losing some games, but I'd like to play well and have fun. It's tough to have fun when you're getting pounded into the hardwood.

Cody coiled his 32-foot, 7/16-inch, medium-soft nylon rope and built another loop. The dirty gray rope circled his straw cowboy hat twice, and then he stepped toward the steer head and let the loop sail straight out and drop around the hard plastic horns. He jerked the rope tight and then walked forward to let his silent prey loose.

"Is that how you get ready for a big game?"

Larry plodded toward him through the pine-tree-covered vacant lots that separated their houses.

"What are those?" Cody pointed to Larry's feet.

"Ankle weights."

"Why are you wearing them?"

"They'll help my feet feel light tonight. I'll be able to jump higher."

"That really works?" Cody asked.

"Eh . . . I don't know. I've never tried them before. But it seems like it should work, doesn't it?"

"Yeah. Let me know if it makes a difference."

Larry started jumping up and down as if he had a jump rope.

"That helps, too?"

Larry smiled. "Yeah. It increases my hang time."

"Hang time? How much hang time can a thirteen-year-old have anyway?"

"You'd be surprised, Cody, my man. But you didn't

answer me. How does tossing that lasso help you play basketball?"

"I don't know. . . . Sort of relaxes me, I guess." Cody
tossed the loop over the plastic steer head again and
yanked the rope tight.

"Don't you ever miss?" Larry asked.

"Nope. But this calf doesn't duck, turn, balk, or break
for the other end of the arena."

"I've been thinking about tonight's game," Larry said
as he watched him build another loop.

"Yeah, I know what you mean. I was just talking to the
Lord about it myself."

"Are you that scared?" Larry asked.

"Scared?"

"Why else would you pray except when you're scared?"

"I guess I sort of talk to the Lord all the time."

"Why?"

"Well . . . 'cause He's like a good friend who's always
there, and I like talking to Him, that's all."

"Man, it's like the whole team is sort of weird. First,
Feather's named by the trees. Then you spend your free
time talking to God. Next thing you know, Jeremiah will
be smearing on war paint before every game."

"Oh, did he tell you about that?" Cody needled.

"You've got to be kidding! I was just joking. Oh, man,
I can't believe—"

"Relax, Larry! I was kidding."

Larry Lewis stopped jumping in place and reached
down and adjusted the ankle weights. "How about you
talking to the Lord all the time?"

"Oh, that part's true. It's a habit I've had for years. My mom says it's because I never had a younger brother to talk to."

Larry jumped in place again. "Hey, you want a younger brother? I'll send Kevin over, and he can stay with you."

"No thanks. I like it the way it is."

"Well, I've got a good feeling about tonight's game." Larry began to hop on one foot and then the other.

"How come?"

"Because Mom is making my lucky lasagna. I always play well when we have that lasagna for dinner. When are we going to go over our plays?" Larry asked. "I think we should meet about six and discuss strategy, don't you?"

"What strategy? All we need to do is score as many points as we can without getting an arm broke. If we stay spread wide, take good shots, substitute often enough to be rested—well, that's about all we can do."

"You're kidding me, right? We've got to run some plays. Some basic pick and rolls, some triangle plays and—"

"Triangle? It's three-on-three. Everything we do is in a triangle!" Cody protested.

"You know what I mean! I think I'll go home and draw us out some new plays." Larry turned back to go across the lots. "If these plays work, you might not need to pray," he called, lumbering back through the trees.

Cody tossed another loop over the steer horns and sighed.

The Halt High School gym hadn't changed much since Cody's dad played center on the Huskies' Idaho State

Runner-up A-3 team of 1967. The cement block building stood like a huge hog, with all the other school buildings huddled around it like piglets. The parking lot was still gravel. The bleachers, both ground level and in the horse-shoe balcony, were small, cramped, narrow, and worn smooth by many generations of Wranglers and Levis. The stage curtains at the far end of the gym hung silent with dust and now-muted lines from a thousand class plays.

It wasn't the best gym in the league.

Some would call it the worst.

But for Cody, it was home. He had made his first basket here. His first free throw. His first three-pointer.

And it was the scene of his first bloody nose. And where his gym shorts got ripped in the fourth grade. And where in the first grade Honey Del Mateo had kissed him on the lips.

It's too bad she moved to Yakima the very next year.

The gym always seemed to smell like a mixture of floor wax, disinfectant, and sweat.

Because they had the early game, there was no one in the stands when Cody pushed open the big double doors. He was hoping it would stay that way.

If no one is watching, maybe the Pirates won't have to show off so much!

Larry Lewis and Feather Trailer-Hobbs were at the far end of the gym in the midst of a heated debate.

"We decided and that's that!" she insisted.

Larry waved his hands at her and at the bleachers. "We didn't decide anything! We merely said that was one idea, but we didn't actually vote on it!"

"What's happening?" Cody prodded as he walked up carrying his small duffel containing an olive green towel and a bottle of orange Gatorade.

"I made shirts for us just like we agreed, and now Larry won't wear his!"

"We didn't agree on this, did we, Cody? We can't wear those. What basketball team ever wore tie-dyed T-shirts?"

"Eh . . . well, we . . . ," Cody stammered.

"We agreed, didn't we?" Feather reached over and shoved a bright red, purple, orange, and yellow shirt into Larry Lewis's reluctant hands.

"It seems like we talked about it and said we'd figure it out later," Cody recalled.

Feather folded her long arms. "Well, this is later."

"If we wear these, we might as well call ourselves the Deadheads," Larry ranted.

"And what's wrong with that?" Feather shot back.

Cody shrugged. "I suppose we could use them until we got some real jerseys. But I like sleeveless shirts or tank tops. You know what I mean?"

"I know. Here," she announced, "I made a sleeveless one for you."

"Oh." Cody glanced down at the white T-shirt covered with splashes of psychedelic colors.

Larry slung his shirt down on the bleachers. "I think we ought to just play shirts or skins."

"Very funny!" she snapped. "Are you going to wear the shirts or not? It took me a lot of time to make these!"

Cody glanced at Feather's gray-green eyes that seemed to beg, *please!*

"Hey, let's do it. You know, until we decide on something else at least. How about it, Larry?"

"Can you imagine Michael Jordan ever wearing a shirt like this?" Larry groused.

"Yep," Cody replied.

Larry sighed and picked up his shirt. "Well . . . just this one time. Maybe it will blind 'em and throw off their concentration! Besides, no one will be watching us anyway."

He and Cody pulled off their T-shirts and put on the new ones. Feather had worn hers to the gym.

"Hey, wow! That's cool."

Jeremiah Yellowboy jogged down to join them.

"You actually like these?" Larry gasped.

"Yeah, they remind me of a dream I had last week."

"A nightmare, no doubt," Larry muttered.

"No. Kind of like the sun coming up over the lake in the wintertime when it's frozen and real cloudy, except in the east where the sun's peeking through with purples, oranges, and yellows."

"Well, whatever. Come on, let's go over our plays," Larry insisted.

"Plays? We need to shoot around a little," Jeremiah replied. "The only play we need is one that keeps us from getting clobbered. Come on, let's shoot."

"Wait! That's not on the warm-up schedule until later!" Larry called.

"I guess it is now," Cody said as he followed Feather and Jeremiah out to the basket.

The game started out well. The Pirates made eight quick points, and the Lewis and Clark Squad hadn't even gotten a shot off yet.

At this rate, we'll lose in ten minutes and be out of the gym before anyone else shows up! Lord, this is not a pretty sight.

Playing half-court, Jeremiah tossed the ball in to Cody, who started to throw it to Larry, who was breaking toward the basket. At the last second J. J. darted in front of Larry. Cody faked the throw and dribbled to the basket himself. With Devin Scott towering in front of him and the sound of Rocky Hammers pounding the flooring behind him, Cody flung a desperate bounce pass back out to Jeremiah, who hurriedly tossed up a three-point shot.

Nothing but net.

"All right!" Larry hollered. "Now we're going! We can beat these guys!"

Jeremiah glanced over at Cody, but neither said a word.

Receiving the inbound pass, J. J. Melton drove straight toward the basket. Larry had the position and crossed his arms to take the charge.

Cody turned and stared. *No, Larry . . . don't . . .*

J. J. lowered his shoulder and ran right over the top of Larry Lewis, having no trouble making the lay-in. Larry flew through the air and slammed, back first, into the foot of the stage behind the basket.

Mr. Rentor, who spent most of his time reading a *Wall Street Journal* that he always carried in his back pocket, blew his whistle and called a charging foul on J. J.

Larry lay on the ground stunned, unable to catch his breath.

Cody tried to help him up. "You all right, Larry?"

He shook his head. Tears formed in the corners of his eyes.

"Way to take it for the team, Larry!" Jeremiah called out, helping Cody lead the battered Lewis to the bench.

"Come on, Feather, we need you now." Cody signaled her.

She threw the ball in to Cody, who passed it quickly to Jeremiah. Immediately the ball flew right back to Cody, who tried to dribble it around Rocky Hammers. It was like trying to get by a brick wall on a dead-end street. Cody flipped the ball back out to Feather, who stood at the top of the key.

Rocky left his position to double-team Feather. But she rocketed a bounce pass to Cody. With Devin Scott guarding Jeremiah wide to the left, Cody was left alone under the basket. He was greatly relieved when his lay-in attempt rolled around the rim and finally dropped into the net.

He and Jeremiah didn't say a word as a scowling J. J. Melton retrieved the ball and headed back across the three-point line.

Don't say anything, Feather!

"Good move, cowboy!" she called to him. "Let's blow it by them again!"

He didn't look her way but jogged out to guard Devin Scott.

J. J. was dribbling toward Feather.

Surely he won't mow down a girl.

She held her ground.

Move, Feather! It isn't worth it! Move!

Just as J. J. lowered his shoulder, Feather ducked low and dove for the ball, coming up with the steal. With a one-hand toss, she flipped the ball out to Cody, who sailed it around to Jeremiah, who immediately bounced it back to Feather standing at the free-throw line. She fired up a high, arching shot over a stunned Pirate team.

Nothing but net.

Cody grabbed the ball and bounced it to Rocky. *Seven to eight? We're actually that close?*

J. J. dribbled slowly toward Feather, this time keeping beyond the three-point line.

"Clark, I thought you had a girl on your team!" J. J. trash-talked.

Cody didn't reply.

"All I see here is a skinny boy with long, ugly hair."

Feather kept guarding him closely but didn't say anything.

"Maybe he should wear a sack over his head," J. J. taunted.

"Knock it off, Melton!" Cody finally complained.

"What did you say?"

Cody stopped and turned toward J. J. "I said . . ."

The words had barely come out of his mouth when he realized that Devin had broken to the basket behind him.

The pass was true.

The shot was easy.

The Pirates led ten to seven.

Jeremiah's pass to Cody was intercepted by Devin

Scott, who bounced it out to Rocky, who shot over the top of Feather's outstretched arms. His shot banked off the glass and roared through the net.

Thirteen to seven.

Feather took the inbound pass and dribbled at Rocky.

"Did you make those shirts?" he baited. "What did you do, swallow a paint kit and then puke it all over some T-shirts? Maybe you should be the Puke Heads! Hey, what do you think, J. J.?"

Feather flung up a shot that Rocky blocked into Devin's hands. Three passes and two shots later, the score was fifteen to seven.

Jeremiah dribbled the ball toward the free-throw line. Then he stepped back to the three-point line. J. J. Melton flew at him, arms outstretched. Yellowboy flung the ball toward the basket and dove out of the way.

Nothing but air.

Devin bounced the ball back out to Rocky, who canned a three.

Eighteen to seven.

Then Cody tossed the ball back to Feather and broke to the basket.

"Ain't no way you can go around me," J. J. baited Feather. "Come on, skinny, try it! I've seen fence posts that looked more like a girl than you do."

"And I've seen cow dung that looked more like a boy than you!"

"Say, what?" J. J. roared.

Feather bounced the ball past an outraged Melton to Cody. Just as he caught the ball, he saw the freshman double up his fist as if planning to slug Feather. With fear in her eyes, she started to back away.

Cody flung the ball as hard as he could two-handed, catching J. J. Melton in the middle of his back. He staggered forward and flung his arm around Feather's neck to keep from falling to the floor. She shoved him off her shoulders and slapped him in the face with a smack so loud that the play ceased at the other end of the gym.

Devin and Rocky ran out to J. J. while Jeremiah picked up the loose ball and tossed it to Cody. He made the lay-in.

"That didn't count! She slapped me!" J. J. protested.

"The basket counted," Mr. Lewis roared from the other end of the court. "You lay a hand on that young lady again, Melton, and your season is over. Do you understand?"

"There's no young lady on this court!" he mumbled in a low voice.

"It's eighteen to nine," she replied.

"You're dead meat, Clark," J. J. snarled.

This time the ball was tossed in to Devin Scott, who drove right at the basket. Cody held his ground and gritted his teeth. One step before impact, Devin pulled up and shot a jumper over Cody, whose hands were at his side waiting for the impact that never came.

Nothing but net.

The whistle blew. "Pirates win twenty to nine," Mr. Rentor announced. The two teams jogged to opposite sides of the gym.

"I'll see you outside, Clark!" Melton screamed.

The Lewis and Clark Squad huddled around Larry.

"You doing all right?" Cody asked him.

"Oh, yeah, I just had the wind knocked out of me."

"Thanks, Cody, for bailing me out." Feather nodded. "Those guys are real creeps."

"Well, let's go face the music." Jeremiah grabbed his blue Gatorade and took a swig. "Maybe if we go out together, it'll be all right."

"I've got to stay here and help my dad," Larry announced.

"Maybe it was just a lot of hot air. Can I go over to your house and wait for my mom?" Feather asked Cody. "I told her if I wasn't in front of the gym, I'd be at your house."

"You did? Oh . . . sure, that's fine," Cody mumbled. "Boy, summer league's starting out with a bang."

"It started with a loss," Larry complained. "I think we might be able to beat them next time."

"I thought we did pretty good." Jeremiah shrugged. "Last year we lost twenty to three, and I had to go have X-rays afterwards."

They had just walked out into the parking lot when Cody heard a voice shout, "Clark, I want to see you over here. Right now!"

Five

●

*A*re you talking to me?"

The voice was deep. Strong. Confident. It seemed to boom across the scattered parked cars. And it was definitely not Cody's.

Denver Clark stepped up alongside his younger brother from behind the pickup. He was six inches taller and eighty pounds stronger than Cody. "J. J., did you say something to me?" Denver called out across the almost empty parking lot.

"Oh . . . eh, hi, Denver. . . . No, I was just going to say something to Cody," J. J. muttered.

"Go ahead and say it!" Denver challenged.

"Well . . . eh, nice game, Cody! You guys played us tough," J. J. stammered and waved with the guarded enthusiasm of a kindergartner on his first day of school.

"Yeah. Thanks," Cody mumbled.

Scott, Hammers, and Melton silently left the parking lot and began walking downtown.

"What are you doing here?" Cody asked with a wide

smile. He could feel every tense muscle in his body start to relax.

Denver leaned against the front of the truck. "Hey, Becky's feeling sick to her stomach, so we decided not to go to a movie. Did I miss your game?"

"Yeah, it was kind of quick."

"Well, you must have done all right. J. J. said you played them tough. He must have been telling the truth, because he was about to clobber you."

"Cody defended my honor," Feather blurted out.

"He did what?" Denver coughed.

Cody looked down at Denver's boots. "Oh, J. J. was trash-talking Feather, so I popped him in the back with the basketball."

"And Feather popped him in the face with the palm of her hand," Jeremiah added. "And they didn't even call a foul. It was awesome . . . really!"

"Sorry I missed the excitement. I guess I missed out all the way around," Denver added.

"Well, actually, I don't have anything to do tonight," Feather piped up.

"What?" Cody questioned.

"I was talking to Denver! You know, just in case he needed someone to go to the movie with. I thought he might like to know I'm available."

"Well, we're just too late now, Feather girl. The show starts in ten minutes, and it takes forty-five to drive to Lewiston. Anyway, sorry I missed your game, little brother."

"I'd say your timing was pretty good," Jeremiah remarked. "I think we were about to get scalped."

Feather's eyes widened.

"I was joking." Jeremiah grinned.

Denver slapped his strong arm around Cody's shoulder. "You came that close to beating them?"

"Not really. They just get ticked real easy."

Jeremiah headed out across the parking lot. "See you guys tomorrow. Same time for practice?"

"Yeah, I guess. Meet at my house, Townie, and we'll all go out together," Cody instructed.

"And I'm going over to your house now," Feather told Denver.

"Why?"

"I need to wait for my mother to come pick me up." She pulled her long brown hair over her shoulder and began to twist it around her fingers.

Cody held the door of the pickup open and let her crawl in first. "I thought maybe your mom would make it to the game," he observed.

"My father is up in the Dixie area for the summer, protesting the logging," Feather explained. "She usually spends a lot of time communing with the trees when he's gone. She probably just got tied up."

Cody lifted his eyebrows. "Tied up?"

"That's a figure of speech, you know."

Denver looked down at Feather and then over at Cody. "Hey, I can give you a ride out to your place. No need to have your mom drive clear to town."

"That would be great," Feather bubbled. "I can show you our tree preserve and everything! We can just drop Cody off and—"

"I think I'll ride out there with you," Cody inserted. "I want to see where you live." There was a sharp jab to his rib cage from Feather's elbow.

Neither of them said another word all the way out to her tepee in the woods.

The next morning Cody was sitting on his front steps eating a bowl of cold cereal when Larry wandered over at about 9:00 A.M. packing his basketball. Bright blue sky stretched above the green pine trees. Small tufts of brilliant white clouds sailed high overhead. The milk was ice-cold because of the frozen blueberries in the bottom of the bowl, and the cereal crunched between his teeth.

"You just having breakfast?" Larry asked.

"Nah, this is a snack."

"You snack on Cheerios?"

"I like 'em." Cody shrugged.

Larry plopped down next to him and dribbled the ball on the ice-damaged concrete step. "Did J. J. give you any trouble last night?"

"He tried, but Denver came by, and he backed down."

"Why do they want to hurt people? That has absolutely nothing to do with basketball," Larry commented.

"I've just been asking the Lord the same thing."

"Did you get an answer?"

"Not yet." Cody stood up, holding his empty bowl in his left hand. "Here comes Townie! As soon as Feather gets here, we can ride our bikes out to the ranch."

"Ride our bikes?"

"Yeah, Mom, Dad, and Denver had to take some year-lings to the sale yard early. So we get to ride bikes. It's not bad. I ride out there all the time."

"I don't really have a mountain bike," Larry admitted. "My bike has narrow racing tires. They don't do very well in the gravel."

"You can use mine. I'll ride Denver's."

"He'll let you do that?"

"Well, he didn't say no."

Cody put his bowl back in the house and sat down with Jeremiah and Larry.

"I say we go look in the woods first thing," Jeremiah suggested. "That is, if the truck's still out there."

"I have to feed the horses first thing," Cody reminded him. "But then we can track it down."

"Do you really think there's something out there in the woods?" Jeremiah asked.

"Probably just someone trying to get that old rig started and went down there to get some water for the radi-ator or something," Cody suggested.

"Oh, sure. They didn't want the water in the stock tank," Jeremiah scoffed. "Come on, Cody. Admit it. This is a real puzzle."

"Well, maybe we'll just find out this morning," Cody replied. He tugged down the back of his white sleeveless Snake River Stampede T-shirt.

Larry stood up and dribbled the ball between his legs. "Why don't we run through half our practice schedule and then go look at the woods. We could really use some work on passing the ball. I watched the Lakeside Loggers last night, and I think we can beat them if we can keep the turnovers down."

"The Loggers? Who's on that team this year?" Jeremiah asked.

"A kid they called Chewy and—"

"Hey, he's my cousin." Jeremiah's wide grin revealed perfectly straight teeth. "I can beat him."

"And a couple of tall, skinny blond-headed guys."

"That's James and Kent," Cody informed him. "Maybe we can beat them."

For almost an hour the conversation bounced back and forth as rapidly as Larry dribbled. They talked of everything from woods to mysteries, defensive basketball to the NBA and the CIA.

"I don't think Feather's going to show. Maybe we should go on," Larry suggested as he yanked up his high white socks.

"Maybe she forgot," Jeremiah surmised.

"Let's ride our bikes out there and get her," Cody proposed. "Maybe they had trouble starting the VW bus. It wasn't running too good the other day."

Overcoming Larry's reluctance, the trio started out on the gravel road leading south from Halt. The former stagecoach road followed the contours of the hills and wound its narrow way through a forest of pines, firs, and cedars. The only traffic turned out to be a logging truck that breezed by with a full load going the opposite direction, leaving a cloud of dust that hung low and filled their lungs.

To reach Feather's place, they turned off the county gravel road and into a narrow dirt lane that consisted mainly of potholes and tumbleweeds. Half a mile farther they came to an old rusted cattle guard with a rope hanging across it and a hand-written sign that read "Trailer-Hobbs Tree Preserve."

Jeremiah peered down a narrow trail that consisted of no more than parallel tire tracks through the forest. "How much farther? I don't see a tepee." His red and black Chicago Bulls tank top hung wet with sweat around his barrel-shaped chest.

"I don't know. We let her out here last night," Cody answered. "Come on, let's see where this driveway leads."

"Are we supposed to go on that? What if someone catches us?" Jeremiah protested.

"Townie, now you know how I feel when we bicycle on tribal land," Cody challenged.

"That's different," Jeremiah asserted.

"That's easy for you, the pride of the Nez Perce Nation, to say. Come on, you guys, push your bikes across the cattle guard, and I'll tie the rope behind us."

The driveway turned out to be a quarter of a mile long, mostly uphill. In a little clearing not much bigger than Cody's front lawn, he spotted a huge white canvas tepee. Chairs, boxes, and various pieces of furniture were scattered about in the trees.

"That's big!" Jeremiah bellowed.

"Hey, Feather!" Cody called from his position on Denver's mountain bike.

"Go knock on the door, Larry, and see if she's ready to go practice."

"Door? What door? There isn't any door," Larry complained.

"Townie," Cody called, "how do you ring a doorbell on a tepee?"

Jeremiah Yellowboy put both his index fingers between his teeth and blew a loud, piercing, shrieking whistle that seemed to rattle the needles of the surrounding evergreen trees.

"You could wake the dead with that whistle." Larry rubbed his ears.

"Maybe they went someplace." Jeremiah shrugged.

"The VW's over there. I don't think they have another rig. Feather?" Cody hollered again.

It came through the trees like a haunting last note on a sad song. "Cody! Up here!"

He turned to Jeremiah. "Did you hear that?"

"I think so."

Cody jumped off his bike and flopped it in the dirt. He jogged around behind the twenty-foot-tall conical tent. "Feather?"

"Up here, Cody! Come and help me!"

He turned to wave at Jeremiah and Larry. "Hey, guys, come on. Feather needs our help."

Cody scurried up the mountainside, leaping over dead limbs and crunching across a shaded bed of dry needles. The odor of pines mixed in with the fresh mountain air made Cody feel as if he could run forever.

"Feather?" he called.

"We're up here!"

An arm waved from behind some boulders.

"We?" Cody hollered as he scampered toward the rocks. "My mother's up here! Can you help me?"

Cody circled the boulders and discovered Feather's mother sprawled on her back in the needles staring with glazed eyes up at the trees. She wore jeans and a Save the Trees black T-shirt, but no shoes, socks, makeup, or jewelry. Her face was pale.

"Is she . . ." Cody could hardly choke out the words.

"She's having one of her bad spells. I need to get her down to the tepee and give her some medicine."

"Bad spells?" He noticed Feather was wearing moccasins that reached almost up to her thin knees.

"It's a long story. I don't want to talk about it." Feather was starting to cry. "Please, help me!"

"Oh, man!" Jeremiah whispered as he and Larry reached the boulders. "Is she . . ."

"She's had a spell, and we need to help Feather get her back to the tepee. You guys pick up her legs. We'll try to lift this end," Cody instructed.

Soon the quartet gingerly hiked down the hill with Mrs. Trailer-Hobbs slung between them.

"What happened anyway?" Larry puffed as he struggled to keep the woman off the forest floor.

"I woke up this morning, and Mother wasn't in bed. Sometimes in the middle of the night when she can't sleep, she'll go for a walk in the forest. If it's mild weather, she might lie down about sunup and take a nap. So I went looking for her."

"She wanders around the forest at night? Barefoot?" Jeremiah quizzed.

"It's our forest," Feather contended. "She can do whatever she wants. But when I found her way up on the top of the mountain, she was in this spell. She needs her medicine."

"Where is it?" Cody asked.

"Down in the tepee."

"Why didn't you go get it and bring it to her?"

"I was afraid of the cougar," Feather admitted.

"Cougar?" Jeremiah almost let go of Mrs. Trailer-Hobbs's leg.

"There were some fresh cougar tracks around where she was lying. We've noticed a cougar in the woods the past couple of weeks. I was afraid to leave her like this up on the mountain."

"Oh, man . . . stalked by a man-eating mountain lion," Larry groaned. "Now this is the frontier!"

They carefully carried Feather's mother into the tepee, which had buffalo robes spread across the dirt floor and scented homemade candles burning in the middle of the room. Cardboard boxes with clothes, dishes, and assorted stuff crowded around the edge.

"Put her over here!" Feather instructed.

Laying the still silent, staring Mrs. Trailer-Hobbs on the dark brown buffalo robe, Cody, Jeremiah, and Larry started backing toward the doorway.

"Do you need me to ride down to the Randolphs' and call 911?" Cody proposed.

"No, Mom doesn't believe in doctors."

"But . . . she takes medicine?" Larry asked.

"It's her own homemade medicine. It always brings her

out of these spells. I give it to her, and ten minutes later she throws up. About an hour later she feels perfectly normal."

"Normal?" Larry whispered. "Is there anything normal around here?"

Feather dug a wire-locked quart jar of black molasses-looking liquid out of a worn cardboard apple box. "It's probably the same kind of thing your family does, isn't it, Jeremiah?"

"My family goes to the BIA clinic." He shrugged, leading the other two back out into the yard.

"Do want us to wait around?" Cody called back to Feather.

"Just a minute—I'll be out. As soon as I get her to swallow this stuff."

The boys walked over to their mountain bikes.

"Is this kind of weird? I mean, I'm new in town," Larry continued, "but this seems weird, doesn't it? Or is it just me?"

"It's different, that's for sure," Cody agreed. "But everyone gets to choose how they live."

There was a deep, gravelly voiced "No!" followed by a loud slap of a hand hitting bare flesh. All three boys turned and stared at the tepee entrance.

Cody was relieved when Feather emerged with a sheepish smile. "Mother took her medicine," she reported. It dawned on him that she wasn't wearing a tie-dyed shirt, but a white lacy blouse and cut-off jeans.

"Can we do anything for you? Do you need us to try to call your dad?" Cody asked.

"No, he doesn't have a telephone, and he wouldn't give

up the cause just for this anyway. Everything's going to be fine now, but I might be a little late for practice. I take it we're riding our bikes out to the ranch?"

"Yeah, but if you need to stay with your mom, don't worry about practice," Cody assured her. Right at that moment he couldn't remember if he had combed his hair today or not.

"No, I'll ride my bike on out to the ranch in about an hour or so . . . honest. Thanks for coming out to look for me, guys." Feather wiped back a tear. "I was praying that you'd come."

"You were?" Cody asked, staring at her narrow eyes.

"Yeah . . . what's the matter? Didn't you think I ever prayed?"

"No, I was just wondering who you prayed to."

A wide grin broke across Feather's face. "I prayed to your God."

"Really?"

"Yes, and I think He listened, don't you?" she asked.

"Yep. I reckon He did." Cody climbed up on his bike. "Listen, you want us to just go ahead and start without you?"

"Yeah, but you can't go look in the woods until I get there."

"Really!" Jeremiah exclaimed. "Are you serious?"

"After all the teasing you've been giving me, I get to be there when you hike into the woods and find that hideous Taco Bell burrito wrapper." She giggled.

"You've got it. We'll see you at the ranch, Feather girl." The name tripped off Cody's tongue. He didn't turn around and look at her because he knew he was blushing.

By the time the boys rode back to town, picked up a basketball, stopped by the Behind the Chutes Minimart for a Coke, and pedaled out to the ranch, it was almost noon. Larry and Jeremiah shot some baskets while Cody went across the road to take care of Eureka Blaine's horses.

When he finished, he stuck his sweaty head under the faucet at the stock tank and let the cold water roll over his neck. Then he took a deep drink and hiked out toward the old pickup, still abandoned in the exact same location.

Lord, if we're going to figure this thing about the pickup out sooner or later, I'd like for it to be sooner.

He routinely checked the locked doors and glanced in at the cab.

"What's it doing back up there?" he mumbled. Then he took off on a sprint toward the road.

"Hey, Townie! Larry!" he hollered as he dashed across the gravel road. Jogging toward the barn, he saw Jeremiah stop and look his way. When he did, Larry broke around him toward the basket and made a lay-in.

Lord, doesn't Larry ever stop needing to win?

"Townie! That sucker's back on the dash!" he puffed, trying to catch his breath.

"What's back on the dash?"

"The pizza. The fake pizza is back on the dash of the old pickup."

"That rubber slice I tossed in the back of the rig?" Jeremiah quizzed.

"Yeah, is that something or what?"

"Let's go see what's down in the woods!" Larry suggested as he dribbled the ball back to them.

"We can't. I promised Feather we'd wait for her."

"What if she doesn't come out?" Larry asked.

"If she's not here by the end of practice, we'll take a look."

"Man, this is weird." Jeremiah scratched the back of his head and tugged up his red nylon shorts. "You know what we need to do? We ought to stay all night here at your barn and take turns watching the truck through binoculars or rifle scopes or something."

"Wouldn't that be cool? Maybe take some pictures!" Cody added. "Denver has a camera with a telephoto lens. Maybe we could use it and . . . but it's not all that strong."

"Anyway, if we saw something," Jeremiah continued, "we could sneak over here and . . ."

"And what?" Larry pressed.

"And get into some serious trouble," Cody mumbled staring out at the blacktop road two miles across the prairie.

"Trouble? I thought you said there's probably an easy explanation for this."

"No, I mean out there." He pointed to the road.

"Hey, here comes Feather," Larry whooped. A bright-shirted bike rider could be seen a mile away. "Now we'll go investigate the woods. Why did you say she was serious trouble?"

"Not Feather but that rig following her."

"It's just an old yellow Jeep, isn't it?" Larry asked.

"Yellow Jeep!" Jeremiah groaned. "You mean like the one that J. J. Melton's brother owns?"

"That's the one. Looks like they're headed down here all right."

"You mean the whole Ponderosa Pirate team's coming here?" Larry gulped.

"Yep."

"You don't suppose they want to play a game of basketball, do you?"

"Nope."

Six

∗

What are we going to do?" Larry's voice sounded as shrill as an alarm clock going off an hour too early.

Jeremiah watched the yellow Jeep pull onto the gravel road. "We could try to outrun them!"

Larry grabbed the basketball and dribbled between his legs. "Oh, sure, they've got a Jeep."

"If we could make it to the trees, they couldn't follow us there." Jeremiah nodded to the evergreen forest a mile east of the barn. "Then if we made it to tribal land and they were still following us, we could scalp 'em."

Larry's chin dropped to his chest. The ball bounced away from him.

"Joking! About the scalping part—not the running."

"But we shouldn't have to run," Cody protested. "This is our ranch. It's private property."

"Swell. We can have them arrested for trespassing . . . if we survive!" Larry grumbled. He picked up the basketball and spun it on the end of his finger.

"You two get in the barn!" Cody ordered, waving his hands toward the big wooden door.

Larry tucked the ball under his arm. "What good would that do?"

"We can at least slow them down. Townie, run back there and close up the back doors. There's a gate latch on the little one and a wooden slide bar on the double door. Larry, get the bikes into the barn!"

Jeremiah darted inside, then called back out, "How about Feather?"

"I'll think of something! After you get that stuff put up, stay out of sight!" For a moment there seemed to be no other sound on earth except Cody's booming voice.

Feather pedaled furiously up the gravel road. The Jeep hung back a few hundred feet and left a trail of dust behind it. Cody heard Jeremiah slam the doors in the back of the barn.

Lord, I'm glad all our horses are out on summer pasture. You know, this would be a really good time to wake up from a bad dream . . . or maybe You could strike them . . . I mean, strike the Jeep . . . a flat! Yeah, maybe they could have a flat. No, then they wouldn't have any way to leave. I changed my mind, Lord. Maybe You could just appear to them as a bright light and convert them all like You did Paul on the road to Damascus. . . . Maybe You want me to figure this out.

Larry pushed the last bicycle into the barn. Cody could see him and Jeremiah peeking out the big front door. "You guys keep out of sight and be ready to bolt that door after Feather gets inside," he hollered. "Toss me that basket-ball." The ball rolled out of the barn from unseen hands.

He dribbled over to the basket and nonchalantly tossed up a quick jump shot.

Nothing but air.

"We've got company!" Feather hollered as she whizzed past the empty corrals and into the yard.

Cody kept shooting, not even looking back at her. "Get off your bike, Feather, and walk it into the barn as if that's what you always do."

"Where's Townie and Larry?"

"In the barn. Have them lock the door as soon as you get inside."

"How about you?"

"I'll stall them for minute. Go on! Make sure every door in that barn is locked."

Feather dismounted and walked her bike to the barn. She disappeared behind the half-open huge double door. Cody fired up another shot as the Jeep pulled into the yard, parking crossways in the lane. J. J., Rocky, and Devin piled out and stalked toward Cody.

J. J.'s brother stayed behind the wheel of the yellow Jeep.

"Clark! It's you and me!" J. J. called out.

"Why?"

"You know why!"

The three boys spread out as they approached. "J. J., you were treating Feather bad, and you know it. That's not right."

"How I treat some skinny, ugly girl is none of your business!"

Cody felt his neck blush with anger. He knew if he

stopped dribbling, his hands would be shaking. He just wasn't sure if it was out of rage—or fear.

"Feather's not ugly. And it *is* my business. She's my friend. You stand up for your friends, don't you?"

Lord, this isn't going very good.

"You slammed a ball into my back."

"Now I'm sorry about that. I shouldn't have done it, but it was the only way I could think of to make you leave Feather alone."

"Well, now, the only way I can get even is to bust your tail," J. J. threatened.

Okay, Lord, now's the time for that miracle.

"I don't want to fight you, J. J." Cody tried hard to keep his voice from quivering. "So why don't you just go on home? You guys are trespassing anyway."

J. J. looked at Devin and then at Rocky. "Yeah, right. But that's not the way I plan on telling it. I'll just say we came over for a basketball game, and the game got a little too rough, that's all."

"Oh? You guys want to shoot some buckets?" Cody still bounced the ball but backed up closer to the side of the barn.

J. J. glanced at the other two, and all three smirked. "Sure, we'll play three-on-one, unless the powerful Lewis and Clark Squad wants to crawl out of their holes."

"I thought you said it was just you and me, one-on-one, J. J.?"

He raised his eyebrows and nodded to the others. "Yeah, that's right. Just you and me and no-rules basketball."

"What do you mean, no rules?" Cody questioned.

"One-point baskets—the first one to ten wins. No other rules."

"Devin and Rocky will stay out of it?"

"I don't need any help beating you! And I do mean beat!"

"Okay, let's get started." Cody spun from where he was standing and tossed in a lay-in. "One—nothing. I'm ahead."

"We haven't started yet!" J. J. hollered.

"Sure we did."

"You didn't bring it in. You didn't check the ball!"

"You said no rules!" Cody grabbed the bouncing rebound and immediately chucked it back up for another easy lay-in.

"What do you think you're doing?" J. J. screamed. "It's my ball!"

"Two—zip. I'm winning!"

"You can't . . ." J. J. ran right at Cody, who grabbed the ball and tried to dribble away from the basket. Strong hands slammed against the middle of his back, and the force of impact caused Cody to trip over the ball and crash into the dirt. He rolled over and quickly tossed a handful of very dry dirt and manure at the diving J. J., who staggered back while rubbing his eyes.

Cody scooped up the ball and ran for the bucket without dribbling, making another lay-in.

"That's three!" he shouted.

"That's traveling!" Rocky sneered, moving a little closer.

"How can there be traveling in no-rules basketball?"

Jeremiah shouted down from the open loft doors. Cody now noticed Feather looking down with him. Jeremiah nodded toward the rope that hung almost to the ground from the big block and tackle.

Cody grabbed the basketball as J. J. cleared his eyes and sprinted toward him. "Here!" Cody shouted. "You can have a shot."

He fired the ball right at J. J., who caught it and flung it thirty yards out into the corral. "I'm through playing basketball!" he shouted.

"Then Cody won!" Feather shouted down.

J. J. stalked toward Cody. "You're dead meat, Clark!"

With a wild leap, Cody caught the dangling rope. Jeremiah and Feather strained to reel it through the pulley, raising Cody to the loft. He dove through the opening just as those on the ground plastered the side of the barn with gravel.

"Are you okay?" Feather asked Cody as he rolled over on his back in the hay and caught his breath.

"Yeah . . . so far." He heard someone rattling the barn doors beneath them.

"That was close, cowboy." Jeremiah shook his head and peeked back out at those below.

"I felt like Daniel being plucked out of the lions' den!"

"Like who?" Feather asked.

"You know—Daniel and the lions' den?"

"In the Bible," Jeremiah added.

"Oh." She shrugged. "We don't have one of those."

"Where's Larry?"

"Over here." Larry Lewis stepped out from behind several stacked bales of hay carrying a ten-pronged muck fork.

Cody heard someone at the back of the barn banging on the door.

"What do we do now?" Jeremiah asked.

"Pray that the doors stay locked," Cody offered. "What are they doing, Townie?"

"Devin and Rocky are back at the Jeep. I guess it's J. J. making all the noise."

They could hear him bang on the barn boards all along the east side of the barn as he ran back to the front. "Clark, you can't hide forever!" he hollered.

Lord, how did I get in this mess? I don't want to fight anybody. I don't want to get mad at anybody. I don't want anybody to get mad at me. How can I get into this much trouble when I'm trying so hard to do things right?

"Do you hear me, Clark? I'll be waiting for you right out here!"

"I hear you, Melton," Cody shouted. "Why don't you just go on home? This can't be so important as to waste a whole morning."

"I'm not going anywhere, and neither are you!" J. J. screamed.

With all of those on the ground huddled around the yellow Jeep, Cody and the others sat down in the loft staring out at the yard. Most days Cody enjoyed sitting in the tall loft, looking out across the prairie at the not-too-distant Bitterroot Mountains.

This was not one of those days.

"What are we really going to do now?" Larry asked.

Cody sighed and shook his head. "I don't know. Sorry about this, guys. It's all my fault."

"Your fault?" Feather crossed her long legs in front of her. "I'm the one that caused it all. I even led them out here. I knew they were back there, but I didn't know what else to do. Cody, thanks for saying I'm not ugly."

He could see a tear trickle down her dusty cheek.

"Oh, man . . . I almost forgot. How's your mom doing?" Cody asked.

"She's just fine. I think she ate some bad mushrooms or something. She doesn't remember anything. I told her about you guys coming out to help."

Cody glanced out at the Jeep and then back at Feather. "What did she say about that?"

"She said that she was glad I had some good friends, but that . . . well . . . that's about all."

"What else?" Cody pressured.

"Oh, you know how moms are. . . . She said she hoped you guys weren't infected with too much chauvinism."

"Infected with what?" Jeremiah gasped.

"Tell her not to worry. We've all had our shots," Cody quipped.

Feather laughed and wiped her eyes on the sleeve of her tie-dyed shirt.

"Did we do something wrong?" Cody could tell he was starting to blush. "I didn't mean anything disrespectful," he mumbled.

"Forget it." She grinned a full-toothed smile. He thought she looked older when she flashed a wide smile. "This really is the boonies, isn't it?"

"I guess so," Cody said, "but I'm really glad your mom's better. Does this happen very often?"

"Nah . . . not more than once or twice a year usually. It's sort of getting routine. Only this time she was so far from the tepee, and that cougar was on the prowl."

"That was really, really scary to me!" Larry nervously pounded his fist with the palm of his hand. "I wish we had the basketball up here. We could run through some passing drills or something."

Cody looked over at Larry's bright blue eyes. "You're serious, aren't you?"

"I'm sort of . . . you know . . . nervous without a basketball around."

"I know what you mean." Feather folded her hands beneath her chin. "I had a blanket that I couldn't live without when I was a kid."

"That's not the same thing at all!" Larry shot back.

"Hey, guys." Cody stood and scooted over to the loft doorway, then came back, and sat next to Jeremiah. "I have an idea. You three could go downstairs and get your bikes. Then while I'm talking to J. J. from the loft door, you could sneak out the back, cut across the bull pen, and ride down the lane to the blacktop. They wouldn't even see you."

Larry's voice got even higher. "Really?"

"How would you get home?" Feather asked.

"Well, maybe one of you could tell my folks where I am when they come home or something."

"We're in this thing together, *amigo*," Jeremiah insisted. "We stick with you—right, guys?"

"Yep." Feather nodded. "Maybe I'll get a chance to use my karate. How about you, Larry? You sticking with Cody?"

"Eh . . . what did you mean, cut across the bull pen? What's a bull pen?" Larry pondered aloud.

"It's a pen where the bulls are kept. They've already done their work, so we separate them out from the cows," Cody explained.

"You mean a pasture full of real bulls?"

"You think he was talkin' about the Chicago Bulls?" Jeremiah teased.

"No, it's just that I didn't know there really was such a thing as a bull pen."

"Now you know," Feather continued. "Are you staying with us?"

"Oh, yeah . . . sure. I'm with you guys."

Jeremiah sat on a bale of hay watching the Jeep. "You really think they'll stay out there very long?"

"I think they'll get bored pretty soon. Don't you think so, Cody?" Larry quizzed.

"I don't have any idea. There's no way I can think like J. J. Melton. I know we'll get bored soon."

"Maybe one of us can sneak down and get the basketball. We really could use more practice on ball handling," Larry insisted.

"What's with you?" Feather grilled. "There's more to life than basketball!"

"Not if you come from Indiana and your dad's the basketball coach. Look, if I don't get a basketball scholarship to a major college, preferably the University of Indiana, it's like a lifetime failure."

Cody whistled between his teeth. "That's a mighty high goal."

"My dad says I have the potential, but I just don't have the discipline yet."

"You don't have the discipline?" Jeremiah crowed. "I've never met any kid who thinks about basketball more than you!"

"Dad knows what he's talking about. He's a good coach. With his help, maybe I'll make it. 'Course, if I could grow a foot taller, it would be a lot easier."

"What do you do for fun, Larry?" Feather asked.

"What do you mean?"

"What do you do besides play basketball?"

"I don't have much time for anything else," Larry replied softly.

"You've got to do something besides play basketball!" she pressed.

"Well, I collect sports cards and—"

"Basketball cards?"

"Eh, yeah."

"That doesn't count as something else."

"Why's everyone looking at me? Why don't we talk about someone else?" Larry pleaded.

Cody glanced back out at the yard. "Okay, Feather, what do you do besides home-school and play basketball?"

"And take care of your mother," Jeremiah added.

"When we lived in Oregon, I took karate lessons."

"Really?"

"Yeah, but I wasn't very good. I guess I spend a lot of time reading. We don't have a television, you know."

"What do you like to read?"

"Mysteries . . . and romances." Her voice trailed off into a soft murmur. "We used to travel all the time. We went to concerts all over the country. And Rainbow People gatherings. But Mom kind of got worn out on those. I've been in almost every state, you know. How about you, Jeremiah? What do you do besides shoot three-pointers?"

"I like to hunt and fish," Yellowboy replied. "Especially with my grandfather. He has a story for every hill and stream in the county. I might go deer hunting with him next weekend."

"Next weekend? Is it hunting season?" Larry asked.

"The season is always open for the Nez Perce."

Larry cautiously peeked out at the Jeep and then sat back down. "Really?"

"Yeah." Jeremiah nodded. "Then I like going down the pow-pow trail."

"The what?" Feather asked.

"You know . . . pow-wows. Where Native Americans get together to celebrate their cultural heritage with celebrations and competitions," Cody explained chewing on a piece of sweet green hay. "Townie's a really good dancer. You ought to see him all dressed out."

"You mean with buckskins and headdress and everything?" Feather quizzed.

Jeremiah's dark brown eyes sparkled. "Yeah, it's a lot of fun."

"They still actually have pow-wows?" Larry croaked.

"About every weekend during the summer, if you wanted to go to them. My cousin Red Hawk had a big travel home. He was full time on the pow-wow circuit until he died in that car wreck."

"Man, I am living in a different world!" Larry rolled his eyes and tilted his head toward the barn roof.

"They're great," Cody added. "You ought to go see Townie dance."

"You mean anyone can go?" Larry started to chew on a straw like Cody but then quickly spat it out.

"Most of the time. Once in a while they're closed to you palefaces."

"I'd like to go sometime," Feather announced.

Cody walked over to the open loft and stared down. "I can't believe they're still hanging around. There's got to be something that we can do."

"Well, you can tell us what your hobbies are besides basketball, calf-roping, and talking to God," Feather teased.

"Oh, nothing special, I guess. I like going to the live-stock auction . . . and rodeos . . . and camping out in the woods." He came back and flopped down on a bale of hay.

"You know what I was thinking?" Feather's voice was soft. She stared down at the thin legs tucked underneath her.

"What?" Cody asked.

"I was thinking that if I'd gone out for the girls' league, none of this would have happened. I mean, no one would have said mean things to me, and Cody wouldn't have blasted J. J., and we wouldn't be up here in the loft hiding."

"Yeah, but if you hadn't done that, we'd never have met Feather Trailer-Hobbs. I'm glad you're on our team." Cody didn't look her in the eyes. "Is it getting stuffy in here?"

"You're turning a little red in the face," Jeremiah teased.

"I am not. It's just warm in here." Cody scooted back to the open loft door.

"They still there?" Larry quizzed.

"Yeah. Hey, here comes somebody down the gravel road!"

"All right!" Larry whooped. Feather and Jeremiah joined them at the open loft.

"Is that your folks' car?" Feather asked.

"No, it's a—it looks like a limo!" Cody reported. "Man, look at that. It's a black limousine."

Feather lifted her long hair off the back of her neck and fanned herself with her hand. "Why are they coming out here?"

"Undoubtedly they're lost," Cody ventured. "Probably want someone to tell them how to get back to the state highway."

"Whoa, look at that!" Jeremiah pointed to the yellow Jeep. "Those guys are leaving!"

"They must think that limo's heading here," Larry surmised.

"Maybe it is." Feather reasoned, "Why else would they be on this road?"

"If they want directions, we ought to say, 'Pardon me, but do you have any Grey Poupon?'" Jeremiah threw his arms around Cody's shoulders and howled.

Cody pulled away. "Yeah, right."

"J. J. is turning back toward town."

"Well, whoever's in the limo, they came along at just the right time," Cody exulted.

"Wait a minute! Look!" Jeremiah pointed. "They stopped over by Blaine's corral."

The quartet boomed in unison, "The old pickup!"

"Come on, let's go check it out!" Cody yelled. He led the charge over several tons of stacked hay, down the ladder, and across the dirt floor to the front door of the barn.

"Hurry!" Jeremiah panted.

"The bar's stuck!"

Feather handed him an old axe handle. "Here, hit it with this!"

Cody banged the bar loose and swung open the door. Fresh mountain air filled his lungs as he took off on a dead run across the yard. Jeremiah and Larry were at his heels.

Suddenly Feather flew past them on her bicycle.

By the time he reached the gravel road, Cody's side ached.

By the time he looked up, the limo was speeding back toward the blacktop road.

"Wait!" he hollered and waved his hands. "Wait!"

The boys reached Feather about the same time. She sat on her bike right where the car had been parked.

"Did you see them?"

"Who was it?"

"What did they look like?"

"What were they doing?"

"Was there only one, or were there more?"

"Did you speak to them?"

"What did you find out?"

"I didn't see anyone do anything," she explained. "When I got here, the limo was pulling away. The back window is tinted."

"You mean you saw absolutely nothing?" Cody asked.

"Well, not completely nothing. I saw the back end of a long black Cadillac."

"Is that it? We could tell that much from the loft," Jeremiah complained.

She pulled on her long brown hair. "Well, there was one other thing."

"What's that?" Cody asked.

"It had a California license plate."

This time it was an excited trio of boys who responded in unison, "California!"

Seven

❖

"What's a limo from California doing in the mountains of north-central Idaho?" Larry pondered.

"What's a limo doing anywhere in Idaho?" Cody could still see the long black rig racing toward town.

"One time when I was in Sun Valley, I saw lots of limos," Feather reported.

"That doesn't count," Cody said. "Sun Valley's not real Idaho. It's too phony. All those rich Californians and movie stars from Hollywood are moving up there and—"

"They were taping a segment of *America's Most Wanted* when I was there," Feather informed him.

"Maybe that's it!" Jeremiah shouted. "All the publicity drove them out of Sun Valley, and the criminals have moved to north-central Idaho!"

"The woods! To the woods!" Cody yelled out, sprinting to the pasture fence.

"What happens if J. J. and the others come back looking for us?" Larry cautioned.

"They won't find us at the ranch, and it's a cinch they

won't find us in the woods." Jeremiah dashed to catch up with Cody.

"Where shall I leave my bike?" Feather yelled out.

Cody was already out by the pickup. "Leave it by Eureka's trailer!" he hollered.

"But what about practice? We haven't practiced basketball yet!" Larry protested.

"I did," Cody asserted. "Come on, Larry, we can practice later."

"You promise?"

Cody didn't answer. He and Jeremiah were trying to find the footprints in the pasture grass they had spotted the day before. Feather scurried to catch up with them.

"Listen," Larry called from the roadway, "I'll be right there. I've got to go and get something! Wait for me to come back!" He sprinted back across the gravel road to the Clark ranch.

"What did he go get?" Feather asked.

Jeremiah glanced back toward the big barn. "Maybe he wanted that pitchfork for protection."

"Chances are he wants to bring his basketball," Cody commented.

"Weird. . . . He's really weird," Feather pronounced.

Cody and Jeremiah glanced at each other and then back at Feather.

"Okay, okay, we're all kind of weird, aren't we?"

"I like to think of it as unique. The Lord makes everyone special and different." Cody grinned in such a way as to reveal a slight scar at the corner of his mouth.

"Are we going to wait for Larry?" she asked. "We could go ahead to the edge of the trees. He can still see us."

"Hey, I think I found the footprints we saw yesterday!" Jeremiah called out from far down the sloping mountainside pasture.

"Wait up." Cody and Feather jogged along together until they caught up with Jeremiah, who stood in the shade of a big aspen tree. Its light green roundish leaves shimmered in the soft summer breeze. The sun was straight above, but it didn't feel hot.

"Look . . . aren't those some fairly fresh tracks heading down that gulch?" Jeremiah pointed to bent grass that looked intertwined on the downhill side.

Cody glanced back toward the old pickup but didn't spot Larry. Then he squatted down to look closer at the tracks. "Someone went down into that brush, all right."

"What's down there?" Feather asked.

"Just a little crick—," Cody started to explain.

"A creek?"

"Same thing," Cody chafed. "There's a spring back over on the mountain on the west side of our ranch. It flows down across this corner of Eureka's place."

"Is it good to drink?"

"If you're a horse or a cow. Here's the number-one rule about drinking from a crick in ranch country: Never drink downstream from the herd."

"Oh, yuck!" Feather gagged. "Are we downstream?"

"Yep. But the guy at that pickup didn't know that. Maybe he came down here to get a drink."

All three stood at the edge of the trees waiting for Larry's return.

"He? What if it's a she?" Feather challenged.

Cody laughed. "Now there's a thought."

"No, really. Why do boys always think it has to be a man who does something mysterious?" she quizzed.

"She's got you dead to right, partner," Jeremiah badgered.

"All right," Cody conceded. "He, she, or it—who has feet bigger than mine—went down the hill right about here."

"Come on, let's see where he, she, or it went," Jeremiah prodded.

Cody looked back at the old pickup once more. "Feather, how about you waiting here for Larry, and then you guys come on down where me and Townie will be—"

"Oh, no, you can't go without me!" She strained her neck and peeked down the mountain into the brush.

"What's keeping him?" Jeremiah pulled up his tank top and wiped the sweat off his forehead.

"He's probably over there shooting baskets!" Feather griped.

Jeremiah said, "Maybe we could just leave a marker here."

"It won't take us long to get down to the bottom of the coulee." Cody stared down the winding, narrow trail. "We could probably make it down there and back up before he even shows."

"Yeah," Jeremiah agreed. "Feather's probably right. He must be over there practicing."

"Pile up some rocks in a little stack. Come on . . . grab those over there," Cody barked the orders.

"Everyone look in the weeds for clues," Feather insisted.

"For dead bodies?" Cody joshed.

"No, for Taco Bell burrito wrappers!" Jeremiah shouted as he plowed down the hill.

"Very funny!" she pouted.

Cody stopped about every thirty yards down the sloping mountain and built up a little pillar of rocks. He always made sure he could see the previous one from the new position.

They followed horse trails through the brush into a small clearing about halfway down the slope. In the middle was a barely used salt block.

"Is this still on Eureka's ranch?" Jeremiah asked.

"Yeah, it goes all the way to the crick. I forgot there's a clearing down here. It's been a long time since I hiked all the way down. Do you see Larry?"

Feather glanced back up the trail. "Nope. I told you he wasn't coming." She slapped at a large mosquito camped on her leg just below the knee.

"The horse trail is packed pretty hard. I can't tell if anyone's been down here or not," Cody admitted. "What do you think, Townie?"

"I can't see fresh tracks. My grandfather's really good at finding sign. Maybe we ought to have him come take a look."

"Does he live in Halt?" Feather asked.

"No, he lives in Nespelem up on the Colville Reservation. But he's coming to see us next weekend."

"Let's just hike down to the crick, look around, and then come back up and find Larry," Cody suggested. "Chances are we aren't going to find anything anyway. Put a marker by that salt block."

The trail to the creek was narrow and steep. There was an overgrowth of green-leafed brush, and Cody felt the scrape of branches etch their presence into his bare legs and arms.

"No one would come down here on purpose!" Jeremiah pronounced.

"It's going to be a steep climb out of here," Cody observed. "Why would anyone want to be down here?"

"To hide something," Feather piped up. "This would be a perfect place to hide a buried treasure . . . or stash illicit drug money."

"Or the drugs themselves," Cody suggested.

"Or a body! Or something worse!" Jeremiah cried. "Look!"

Cody felt his heart jump. "What is it?"

"Ah, hah. This land is not as primitive as you might think!"

"What is it, Townie. What do you see?"

"Is it gross? I don't want to look if it's gross," Feather announced.

Jeremiah dropped to his bare knees and scraped back some dirt with his hands.

"Yes . . . here it is. Look. A genuine hood off of a Model

T Ford! It's buried right here in the dirt on the side of this draw."

"Townie! You got us all worked up," Cody chided.

"It's just a pile of junk," Feather commented after examining it.

"Junk?" Jeremiah protested. "This could be a valuable antique. There are people who would pay good money for this!"

"Why?"

"Well, maybe there was a car wreck here years ago, and someone famous died. And they've never found a trace of him! Hey, let's dig around and see if there are any bones!"

"That is gross, Yellowboy . . . very gross," she muttered.

"Someone pushed an old junker over into a ravine to get it out of sight. Big deal," Cody declared. "Come on, let's get down to the crick and back up before Larry misses us."

The trail steepened right before it reached the creek. Cody led the way to the bottom where the brush opened up into a small meadow of green pasture grass irrigated by the meandering five-foot-wide creek.

Jeremiah wandered along the creek bank, peering in the grass. "Okay, we've made it to the crick, partner. Now what?"

"I don't see anything," Feather reported. "What are we looking for anyway?"

"I don't know," Cody admitted. "It doesn't look like any-one's been tramping around in the grass, does it?"

"Nope." Jeremiah continued to scout the grass and brush. "All right!" he hollered as he pounced on an object stuck back in the brush. "I found it!"

"Another piece of car junk?" Feather sneered.

"No, this is really it. It proves our earlier theory. Look!" He held up what remained of a large white paper cup. "It's a KFC cup! Isn't that what we expected?"

Cody laughed and shook his head. "No, we were looking for a Taco Bell burrito wrapper."

"This is close. The same guy who had the burrito at Taco Bell stopped at Kentucky Fried Chicken and bought a drink!"

"That cup looks three years old!"

"So did that fake pizza in the car. They probably buried the money from the bank robbery down here. Too bad we didn't bring a shovel."

"That's really dumb, Townie," Cody countered.

"Thank you, thank you. You're right. Let's get out of here and go play some basketball. I don't think the people with the pickup even came down this far," Jeremiah agreed.

Feather glanced around at the brush and trees that lined the walls of the ravine. "Yeah, well, it's sort of a nice private hideaway that no one knows about. It's like having our own secret place."

"Why would we want a secret place?" Cody asked.

"Brother!" she moaned. "You have the imagination of a . . ."

"I know. I know—the imagination of a slug. Let's slither up the trail." Cody held out his hand to Feather.

"What's that for?" she demanded.

"What?"

"You want to hold hands with me?"

Cody could hear Jeremiah begin to laugh.

"No . . . I thought . . . I mean, it's so steep I thought you needed some help."

"Oh, sure, but you didn't offer a hand to Jeremiah. That's exactly what my mother warned me about."

"But I didn't do anything!" Cody pleaded.

"I'm quite able to take care of myself!"

Cody turned and sighed.

Soon the trail narrowed and steepened, and they went single file, with Jeremiah taking the lead. In some places, where the footing was loose gravel, Cody crawled up the hill on his hands and feet.

"Cody, I really think you and me ought to camp out at the barn some night and keep an eye on that pickup," Jeremiah called back.

"Well, if we do, we better do it pretty soon. Any day now that truck will be gone."

"Do you think your folks would let us?" Jeremiah asked.

"I think so. 'Course, I wouldn't want J. J. and those guys to know we were at the barn."

"You think Larry would want to come?"

"Well, we could ask him if—"

"Jeremiah!" Feather's voice sounded distant and desperate.

Both boys turned around and glanced back down the steep trail.

"Jeremiah," Feather hollered, "can you help me?"

She was on her hands and knees in the dirt, holding

on to a bush in order to keep from sliding back down the trail.

They rushed back to her.

"Here, grab my hand!" Cody braced himself and then reached his hand down.

"Jeremiah can help me, thank you."

"Hey." Jeremiah shrugged. "The women always go for me. What can I say? It must be my bronzed body."

"Okay, okay, you're both jerks. So why don't both of you help me?" she called out.

Cody grabbed one hand, and Jeremiah held on to the other as they lifted Feather up the trail and tugged her on up to where the steep trail was more manageable.

Cody was surprised how strong a grip Feather had. Her fingers were thin and a little grimy, but they felt warm.

"You can turn loose of my hand now!" she demanded.

Cody realized he was the only one still tugging her along. He immediately dropped her hand and hurried up through the trees, trying not to think about how red his face must be.

All three were out of breath when they made it back up to Eureka Blaine's pasture. They walked slowly around the corral and over to the trailer house where Feather retrieved her red bicycle.

"That was sort of a wasted hike. I guess we better get over there to the barn. Mr. Basketball will dock us for being late for practice," Cody bantered.

"Sometimes thinking about something is more fun than doing it," Feather mused as she rode her bicycle alongside the boys.

"Are you talking about basketball practice or the hike?" Jeremiah inquired.

"The hike." She scowled. "I mean, it was fun to think about some big adventure waiting in the woods. The thoughts were more exciting than the reality."

"You ever notice how lots of movies and TV shows are that way? You think it's going to really be good, and you wait for days or weeks to see it, and then it turns out bad." Cody stared across the gravel road at the barn all the time he was talking. "I guess that's what I like about my faith in the Lord. It's even better than I thought it would be." He pointed to the barn. "I don't see Larry. Do you guys see him?"

"Maybe he's in the barn," Feather suggested.

"Why?"

"Maybe he got tired of waiting and went home," Jeremiah countered.

"He wouldn't do that, would he?"

"It's after lunchtime. He might be hungry," Feather surmised.

Cody and Jeremiah jogged past the corrals and into the Clark Ranch yard with Feather pedaling beside them.

"Larry?" Cody yelled. "Hey, Larry!" He stood in the middle of the dirt yard, eyes searching the horizon. "Townie, go see if he's in the barn. He wasn't over by the pickup, was he? I mean, I didn't actually look over there by the rig."

"I'll ride back over and check it out," Feather offered. Not waiting for a reply, she stood on the pedals and cranked up some speed as she left the yard.

Cody meandered to the east fence and gazed toward

the blacktop road. The slightly worn Rawlings NCAA Final Four indoor/outdoor basketball no longer lay in the grazed short grass of the pasture where J. J. had flung it an hour before.

Jeremiah trotted over to him. "He's not in the barn, Cody. Not unless he's hiding. He's not the kind that would hide, is he?"

"I don't think so. . . . Is his bike still there?"

"Yep. All three bikes are there."

"He's not over at the pickup," Feather hollered as she cruised back into the yard.

"Well, he can't just disappear!" Cody insisted.

"Maybe someone came by, and he went with them," she suggested.

"Who?"

"You know, his mom."

Jeremiah stood on the bottom rail of the fence and was instantly taller than Cody and Feather. "Or J. J. and those guys!"

"Or the big limo. Maybe they came back and kidnapped him," Feather put in.

"And transported him up to an alien spaceship that even now hovers over the planet, where they will reprogram his mind to think of nothing but . . . football!" Jeremiah grinned from ear to ear. "Is that cool or what? Can a slug come up with something like that? I think not."

"I have to admit, one of you is getting better," she gibed.

"Yeah, well, all of this talk hasn't helped us find Larry. If he's not here and he didn't go home, he must have tried to find us. Maybe he went down another trail."

"There's more than one trail over there?" Feather asked.

"There are stock trails crisscrossing the entire ravine. And with the brush grown up like it is, it would be easy to be down in there and not be able to see someone else."

"You mean, we need to hike back down there?" Feather asked.

Cody headed toward the gravel road. "Come on, team, we've got to find Captain Larry Bird Lewis."

"I'll put my bike in the barn and catch up with you guys," Feather called.

"We'll wait for you," Cody told her. "No more of this catch-up-with-us stuff. That's how we lost Larry . . . or he lost us."

They climbed the corral fence at Blaine's and once again hiked out to the old pickup.

"Look, you can see that pile of stones from here." Cody pointed toward the north edge of the pasture. "He knew we were headed that way."

They plodded north. Jeremiah stopped and pointed down to the short grass. "Look at that print."

"I don't see anything," Feather called out. "What is it? What are we looking at?"

Cody squatted down next to Jeremiah. "See that mashed circle?" He pointed to flattened grass.

"Well, it doesn't look like a footprint," she asserted.

"Nope. Looks like a basketball was bounced here, doesn't it?"

Jeremiah brushed a bright blue crawling bug off his

brown leg. "That's exactly what I was thinking. Maybe we can track Larry by looking for where he bounced the ball."

"How do you guys know all this about following tracks?" Feather asked.

"Didn't you know? Boys are just born with this knowledge," Jeremiah teased.

She stuck out her tongue at both of them.

The imprint of a bounced ball was fairly easy to follow in the pasture, but it was downright simple to trace in the dirt and dust of a stock trail.

"It's Larry's expensive shoes, too. Look at this track!" Jeremiah blurted out as he pointed out the mark in the dirt.

"Here's where he took the wrong trail." Cody pointed. "We went down that one over there."

"Where does this one lead?" Feather asked.

"I don't know. Come on, Sacajawea. We've got to find Captain Lewis."

The stock trail switched back and forth several times in the thick brush. There weren't as many exposed boulders and thick brambles as in their earlier trail. They were hiking east down a gradual slope when they rounded a turn and burst upon a clearing. It was mostly dirt, except for a large round patch of short prickly pear cactus.

And a boy sitting on his basketball.

"Larry!" Cody called. "Are you all right?"

"Actually, I'm getting kind of bored. What took you guys so long? Man, I've been waiting for you for half an hour. Did you get lost or something?"

"What do you mean, lost? You were the one who got lost," Jeremiah told him.

"Lost? Isn't this where you said you were going?"

"Eh . . . where are we?" Feather asked.

"Where the people with the pickup came. Didn't you say that's where you were headed?"

"Yeah, but how do we know this is where they came?"

"That's obvious, isn't it. Look!" He pointed to the west end of the cactus patch.

"A tombstone?"

"It's a grave!"

Cody stooped to stare at the grave marker. "Someone must have planted the cactus on top of the grave."

The headstone was no more than a chunk of concrete with some faded black painted words on it.

"I can't make it out. What does it say?" he asked.

"'God is just,'" Larry replied.

"Just what?" Feather quizzed.

"God is just. You know, He's fair," Cody explained. "He can be trusted."

Feather wrinkled her nose and frowned. "That's a strange thing to put on a grave marker."

"Maybe so," Cody said with a shrug, "but there are lots of trails over here. We just hiked on one down to the crick and didn't find anything at all. How do we know someone from the pickup came down here?"

"Because of what's in here!" Larry held up a small round plastic container.

"What's in that?" Jeremiah asked.

"A roll of undeveloped film!"

Feather stepped closer. "Really?"

"Yes, and look at its date."

"That's this year!" she shouted.

"Bingo! I figure it dropped out of someone's pocket, and they don't know where it is."

"And if we develop the pictures," Cody exclaimed, "we can find out what's going on over here!"

Eight

Cody Clark had a serious problem.

Halt, Idaho, boasted a small supermarket, a hardware store, a variety store, a meat market, a lumberyard, a tractor and farm implement business, two minimart gas stations, two huge grain elevators, one very old motel, a bowling alley (closed), four churches, a school (K-12), a library, a city hall, a feed store, a fire station, a blacksmith shop (also closed), six cafes, and twelve bars. But it did not have a one-hour film developing facility.

All important shopping had to be done in Lewiston, Idaho, which was almost forty miles and 3,000 feet lower elevation to the northwest of Halt.

Cody was in the backyard roping his plastic steer head right before dark when Denver came out to get in his pickup.

"Cody, keep that right elbow up a little higher. . . . That's the way. You throw with your arm on an angle like that, and you'll only catch one horn," he instructed.

"Yeah, I know. I wasn't concentrating very much," Cody admitted.

Denver strolled over next to him. He wore his good Resistol cowboy hat and his new lace-up Justin ropers.

"You going out?" Cody asked.

"Becky's feelin' better, so we're headed to the movie."

"In Lewiston?"

"Yeah. What's eatin' at you, little bro?"

"Oh, nothing."

"Listen, when you leave the supper table before dessert and come out here to rope, I know something's wrong. You still thinking about J. J. last night? Hey, relax. He's probably all over that by now."

"They came out to the ranch today, Denver."

"J. J., Rocky, and Devin?"

"Yeah."

"Did they hurt you?"

"Nah. I ran and hid in the barn."

"That's okay."

"I didn't like having to do it. It's not fair."

"Did you tell Mom and Dad?"

"No, they wouldn't understand. They'd probably say it was my fault in the first place and make me apologize. I already told him I was sorry for clobbering him in the back."

"Did you talk to the Lord?"

"Yep."

"What did He say?"

"He said I should 'live in peace with all men as much as I am able.' But I'm not sure I'm able to live in peace with J. J."

"Keep asking the Lord," Denver urged. "He'll show you a way. In the meantime, let me know if they are bothering you. I can go pay them a visit."

"I've got to learn to take care of my own problems." Cody coiled the rope, built a loop, and then tossed it over the steer head.

"I know what you mean, partner. It's not easy being thirteen, is it?"

"Nope. Is it easy being seventeen?"

"Only when you have a date with Becky!" Denver grabbed him around the shoulders and gave him a tussle. "Can I get anything for you in town?"

"Hey . . . yeah. Could you get a roll of film developed for me at one of those one-hour places?"

"Sure. What did you take a picture of?"

"I don't know. See, we found this roll of film out in the trees near Eureka's place. And we were wondering what was on it. It might have a clue to a mystery."

"Oh, yeah?" Denver winked. "And maybe it's someone's vacation pictures. Anyway, it will be easier to give it back to them if we know who it belongs to."

"That's what I was thinking."

"Sure, go get the film. But I'll be real late getting home, so I'll just lay the pictures on your dresser."

Cody lay in his bed and gawked at the red fluorescent dial of his alarm clock.

10:52.

When Denver said "real late," did he mean twelve? Or

one? Or later? I don't think Mom and Dad let him stay out past one even in the summer. I ought to just go to sleep. We've got a basketball game tomorrow night, and I've got to feed the animals early, and Mom said the lawn needs mowing, and . . .

If I got up real early, I could ride my bike out to feed the horses and just hang around Eureka's about sunup. Maybe the limo or whoever would show up.

Of course, maybe J. J. would show up.

Lord, I just don't know what to do about J. J. and the others. I just wish they would go away. Like maybe he'd move to Montana or something.

I can't figure out why it seems to make some people feel good to treat others so bad. You're probably wondering the same thing.

Lord, I really want to do the right thing.

If I can ever figure out what it is.

At least, summer vacation hasn't been boring so far.

10:59.

That's not right, is it? Maybe my clock's broken. It's got to be later than that. Is that a car in the driveway? No, that's over at Larry's. Denver won't be home until late.

I might as well take a little nap and wake up later.

6:01.

Cody's feet hit the brown carpet in his upstairs bedroom before his eyes had completely blinked open. He knocked over a small glass cowboy boot full of pennies and stubbed his toe on a twenty-pound iron dumbbell and then hopped around the room clutching the thick white envelope marked L-C Valley One-Hour Photo. Finally, he collapsed on his bed, rolled to his back, rubbed his toes, and slowly opened the package.

The first picture showed the old pickup in Eureka Blaine's pasture.

So the film is connected to the pickup! All right!

The second photo was also of the pickup. It was a slightly different angle, a little brighter sun.

The third through the twenty-fourth photos were also of the pickup. Front, left side, right side, rear, diagonal, long angle, up close, distant, bright sun, early morning gray, sunset.

Always just the old truck.

Always right there in Eureka's pasture.

Nothing else.

Photo #25 showed the cactus patch down at the clearing in the ravine. The same was true of #26-29. Photos #30-34 showed the faded concrete headstone, "God is just," in several different views.

Photo #35 was solid black.

And #36 . . . *All right! Who's that guy? Bruce? Bruce who?*

Cody eyed a man wearing jeans and a jeans jacket standing beside the driver's door on the old pickup. He held a cardboard sign in front of his face. On the brown cardboard someone had written "Bruce."

That's it? I can't even see his face. Who is this guy besides someone who lost a roll of film? Maybe he'll come back looking for the film!

*The chores! I've got to get out there and feed the horses.
. . . Maybe he's out there now!*

In the town of Halt, it's called First Street. Outside the
city limits, it's known as County Line Road. In either place,
it's the only paved road on the west side of the prairie,
other than Highway 95. Cody pedaled through town,
happy to see no one out and about except for the usual
crowd having breakfast at The Crossing Cafe.

It was Cody's favorite time of the day in the summer.
The air was cool enough at 4,000 feet elevation for him to
wear his National Finals Rodeo zip-up sweatshirt. But the
sky was blue and clear, and the air—as always—was clear
and clean-tasting. The rolling prairie north of town had
challenged him when he was young, and before he bought
himself an eighteen-speed mountain bike.

*I'll just walk up to them and say, "I'm looking after the
stock while Mr. Blaine is gone. I was . . . eh, I was planning
on turning out the broodmares into this pasture today. Will
you have this truck moved soon?"*

*Maybe I could just shout, "Hey, this is private property.
What are you doing out there?" But that might make them
angry. Who knows—maybe they are doing something ille-
gal and don't want any witnesses.*

*I think I'll just go about my feeding chores and check
them out for a while. Then, after I'm done, I'll walk out there
and act real cool.*

Dream on, Clark.

Well, maybe I can at least keep from doing something absolutely dumb.

Maybe.

The first thing Cody noticed when he pulled onto the gravel road back to the ranch was that there was no one at Eureka Blaine's ranch. No limo. No car. No person. No movement. No nothing.

The second thing he noticed was that Two Doc Barb was munching on Vernon McKensie's green oat field. Two Doc Barb was one of two stallions that Eureka Blaine kept around the ranch for breeding purposes. The horse was supposed to be in a five-rail pasture right behind Blaine's ancient, unpainted barn.

Lord, he's the meanest horse Eureka owns. Why is he the one that broke out? Oh, man . . . I wish Denver was out here or Dad or even Mom!

Cody discovered a gate open on the pasture. Sunny Boy Blue, the other horse to share that pasture, was eagerly waiting at the feed trough, content to ignore the escape route.

After closing the gate, Cody fed the remaining horses and trotted across the lane to the Clark barn to get a headstall and lead rope.

Somebody left that gate open. Maybe I should put a note on it that reads: "Shut the gate, Bruce!" Lord, if Two Doc breaks toward the middle of that field, there's no way I can run him down! And if he runs at me . . . This is not fun. This is definitely not fun.

It was a half-mile hike down to McKensie's oat field. Two Doc kept grazing as Cody approached, but he could tell that the seventeen-hand horse was watching him closely. Cody walked slowly, the headstall and lead rope looped over his left shoulder.

"Two Doc, you listen to me," Cody said softly, yet firmly. "You know you aren't supposed to be down here. You're supposed to be up there with Sonny Boy. Now he's missing you, and there's feed in your trough that's bound to taste a whole bunch better than this. So you just stand right there and let me slip on this headstall and . . ."

When Cody came within three feet of the horse's head, Two Doc took a couple of steps backward through the fifteen-inch oats.

"Whoa!" Cody called. "Don't you do that on me. And here I carried a pocketful of sweet oats for you. Come on, boy . . . come on . . . time to go home!"

Two Doc extended his huge muscular neck as far as it would go in Cody's direction without moving his hooves.

"Well, come on, you got to do a little something for yourself. . . . Come on . . . get out of Mr. McKensie's field. That-a-boy . . . one more step."

The horse glanced behind him.

"No, you don't want to run back there. Come on . . . get your oats, and let's go home!"

The big horse took another step toward Cody, opened his mouth, and bit at the air.

"Come on . . . a little more."

This time Two Doc stepped close to Cody and began to eat the oats in his hand.

"That-a-boy. That's good!" Cody stroked the sorrel horse's neck. "Okay . . . now let's put a necklace on you."

With his left hand he laid the lead rope over the top of the horse's neck and clutched both ends of the inch-thick dirty blue nylon rope. Two Doc Barb instantly reared up. Cody clutched the rope with both hands and was lifted off his feet.

"No! Two Doc, no!"

The horse settled back down.

"That's a good boy. . . . Now let's just get your head-stall on and—"

The horse yanked back at the sight of the headstall. The rope burned Cody's hand a little as he grabbed it tight to keep it from being wrenched away. Reaching up with his right hand, he shoved the last of the sweet oats into Two Doc's mouth and then looped one end of the rope over the other, forming one-half of a granny knot under the horse's neck. Still holding on to both ends, he led Two Doc out of McKensie's field.

If he pulls back, I can't hold him like this, Lord. Then I'll be in worse shape than before. It's kind of like looping three legs on a calf only one time before you tie the hooey. You keep thinking surely he'll kick free.

"Just keep walking, big boy. You're doing good. Come on!"

Cody got the horse out to the gravel road and then began the uphill hike to Blaine's driveway.

"'Good-bye, old paint, I'm leavin' Cheyenne . . . off to Montana for to throw the hoolihan,'" he sang.

Soft and low.

Over.

And over.

And over.

All along the way he expected Two Doc to bolt.

All along Cody sang.

Until he walked the big horse into the corral with Sunny Boy Blue and shut the gate behind them.

Then he quit singing.

And whooped.

Wearing a sleeveless tie-dyed T-shirt, Cody entered the Halt High gym about half an hour before game time. He sat in the bleachers watching two other games. He had just determined that the Lewis and Clark Squad could probably hold their own against all of them when Jeremiah Yellowboy bounded into the gym and up into the bleachers and flopped down next to him.

"Hey, Townie, guess what I got?"

"A twelve-foot jump shot that never misses?"

"Dream on! No, really, I've got the pictures!"

"You got them developed? What do they show?"

"Almost nothing. Where have you been all day?"

"Cutting wood with my brothers. Where are they? Let me see them."

"There's two dozen shots of the old pickup at every angle imaginable."

"That's all?"

"And a dozen of the cactus patch and tombstone."

"So they are connected!" Jeremiah sorted through the photos quickly. "What did you mean, almost nothing?"

"Well, take a look at the guy in the last picture."

"Bruce? Bruce who? The sign covers up his face."

"I have no idea."

"That's it?" Jeremiah quizzed.

"Not only that, but I went out to the ranch early, and no one came by."

"So we really don't know anything."

"Not yet, but here's the good news." Cody slapped Jeremiah on the back. "Mom and Dad said we can camp out at the barn if we want to."

"When?"

"Tonight after the game. Can you do it?"

"Yeah!" Jeremiah shouted. "That will be so cool!"

"Don't you have to ask your mom?"

"Nah. She never minds having someone out of the house." Cody waved at another tie-dyed shirted boy dribbling a basketball toward them.

"Here comes Larry!" Jeremiah exclaimed. "Is he staying out there with us?"

"Yeah, I asked him this afternoon. He already has a practice schedule for us tonight."

"Tonight? After the game?"

"Yeah, he says it doesn't get dark until 9:30, so we should have at least an hour to practice. Can you believe that?"

"From Larry? Yeah, I believe it."

"I think we can take these guys tonight. My mom fixed

my lucky pie," Larry announced as he dribbled his way up the bleachers.

"Lucky pie?" Cody laughed. "Is that any better than your lucky lasagna?"

"My lucky what? I don't have any lucky lasagna. At least, not anymore." Larry turned to Jeremiah. "You coming out to the barn tonight?"

"Yep!"

"The great Bruce hunt!" Larry spun the basketball on the middle finger of his right hand.

"How about Feather?" Jeremiah asked.

"We can't have a girl camp out with us," Larry declared.

"Yeah, but Feather's . . . not really like a girl . . . girl," Jeremiah stammered. "I mean, she's not like other girls."

"Well, don't tell her that," Cody warned. "She's liable to bust your nose or something."

Larry sat straight up, the ball under his left arm. "We can beat the Lakeside Loggers if we keep running all night. They aren't in too good shape."

"They look pretty big to me," Jeremiah commented.

"But they can't run," Larry insisted. "Here comes Feather. . . . Let's go over this game plan I've prepared."

"Game plan?" Jeremiah groaned.

Cody just looked up at the 200-watt lightbulbs that lined the ceiling and sighed.

Larry's plan turned out to be a good one, and Cody was surprised at how quickly they jumped out to a fifteen to seven lead. By rotating every two minutes, they all kept fresh and seemed to throw the Loggers off guard. Larry made most of the points and was in a world of his own.

Jeremiah had just come in for Larry and passed the ball in to Cody, who tried to go up for a lay-in but was shoved by a Logger. The shot went long off the glass. Feather flew through the air, grabbed the rebound, and wildly flung the ball toward the basket. It hit extremely high on the glass, bounced twice on the front of the orange rim, and then collapsed into the net.

"Nice shot!" Cody yelled.

"Yeah. I meant to do that!" She shook her head and ran out to guard one of the Loggers.

"Let's get the ball back and shoot a three. Then we can go out to the barn early! Pass me the ball. I feel lucky," Jeremiah announced as they tried to set up some kind of defense.

"What do you mean, barn? Are we going out there tonight?" Feather asked, while keeping her eyes on the kid she was guarding.

Cody glared at Jeremiah, who grimaced and tried not to look at Feather.

She stopped guarding her man, jammed her hands on her hips, and stared Cody down, "I said, are we going out to the ranch tonight?"

The Lakeside Loggers made an easy two-pointer. They bounced the ball out to Feather, who was standing at the top of the key.

"You didn't answer me, Cody Clark!" She checked the ball.

"Let's finish the game," he mumbled.

Feather pivoted toward the basket and hurled up a bullet of a shot that slammed against the glass and plunged through the center of the net.

"There . . . the game's over. Now don't give me a bunch of garbage about you guys staying at the barn tonight without me."

Nine

�֎

I say we post one of us in the loft with the binoculars to keep an eye on the old pickup at all times," Jeremiah suggested.

Larry dribbled the ball around the stack of sleeping bags, snacks, and pillows. "We can see it from here, so we might as well just run through our practice schedule."

"Either way, let's get all our gear moved into the loft." Cody grabbed a green bag and hiked toward the barn.

"Too bad we don't have a night scope." Jeremiah snatched his stuff and hurried to catch up with Cody. "You know those infrared scopes that see at night? I saw one in the catalog for only $350."

"No one's going to come out here after dark, are they?" With a sleeping bag and pillow under one arm, Larry dribbled toward the barn.

"I don't think anyone will want to stumble around after dark." Cody tossed his bag up into the loft and then climbed the ladder, packing the sack of goodies.

"Yeah, if they show up then, they'll have to have a

strong flashlight. We should be able to spot that all right."
Jeremiah huffed his way up the ladder behind Cody.

"Unless we're all sleeping when they come." Larry
flung his gear up to Cody and stayed down on the dirt floor
of the barn to dribble the ball. A fine dust fogged up on his
long white socks. "We ought to make a rotating schedule
for who stays awake and who sleeps. You guys want to
make the schedule, or do you want me to?"

Cody and Jeremiah looked at each other.

"Definitely you make the schedule, Larry," Cody
offered. "No one can make schedules quite like you."

"Yeah, it's a gift, you know. I'll do it right after practice."

"Are we really going to practice?" Jeremiah moaned.
"We just won a basketball game. Isn't that enough for one
night?"

"Hey, listen up," Larry began. "I figured a way we can
play better defense."

"I thought we did pretty good." Jeremiah plopped
down on a bale of hay and stuck a short piece of straw into
his mouth.

"Yeah . . . well, pretty good is not going to win the
championship."

"Championship? Is that what we're supposed to do?"

"What else did you think this summer league was all
about?"

"Fun and recreation?" Jeremiah countered.

"Learn a few skills?" Cody added.

"No! The whole reason we're in this three-on-three
league is to win the championship! Come on, guys, let's
practice while there's still daylight."

"Maybe Feather was the lucky one," Jeremiah grumbled.

Cody started to climb down the ladder. "Well, don't tell her that. She was really, really ticked."

"Oh?" Jeremiah laughed. "What gave you that idea? Was it when she threw Larry's basketball down First Street?"

"I think it was when she kicked over the trash can at the park and left us to pick up the garbage."

"You don't really think she'll quit the team like she said, do you?" Larry asked as the other two reached the ground.

"I don't know, but I hope not. She's a good player." With the sun getting low in the west, Cody considered pulling on his sweatshirt but decided not to. All three were still wearing their tie-dyed game jerseys. "Well, coach, what do we start with? I'd like to practice putting the ball back up after a missed shot."

"I want to practice three-pointers," Jeremiah insisted.

"This is exactly why I need to be the one who lines out the practice schedule." Larry pulled a small folded piece of white paper from his back pocket. "We're going to start with some ball-handling and running drills."

Jeremiah rolled his dark brown eyes. "You've got to be kidding!"

"No, really. It says so right here on the list . . . see?" Larry held the paper in their faces.

"Fourteen different drills? You want us to do fourteen drills tonight?" Cody choked.

"Yep." Larry grinned. "I'm going to see that we do every last one of them."

And he did.

The western horizon reflected a deep burnt orange behind the pine and firs that crested the mountain west of the barn. Up above, the sky was turning a swarthy eternal blue like the last curtain to be raised before the main performance. Within seconds after the sun's descent, the air began to cool.

From a distance it was a portrait of serene contrasts. To the south, Black Angus cattle grazed on grass still tall and green. Dominating the man-made landscape, a huge faded red barn loomed above the series of worn wooden corrals, loading ramps, and squeeze shoots. Towering above the buildings, a windmill water pump, long-neglected, fins missing, sagged under the weight of 100 years.

Everything was quiet . . . pastoral . . . a classic Western painting of a world settling in for a long night's rest.

Except . . .

Except there were three boys frantically catching, dribbling, throwing, running, jumping, and even sometimes gracefully flinging a round synthetic leather basketball at an orange metal ring mounted on the side of the barn, from which a loosely woven white net waited patiently upon the skill and luck of the combatants.

And if Cody Clark, Larry Lewis, and Jeremiah Yellowboy could have stepped back far enough to see the entire countryside, they would have spotted someone pushing a red bicycle through the pasture straight up to the back of the big barn.

If they hadn't been so caught up with a play Larry labeled Hoosier #12, they might have noticed the front door of the barn silently and slowly close.

But what they saw was a hoop, a ball, and a couple of teammates. They could smell the dust fog up in the clean mountain air and feel the chill of a sweaty tie-dyed shirt as it first clung, then rubbed raw on their backs.

"Hey, did you bring some Gatorade?" Jeremiah asked. "I meant to bring some."

"Yeah, I've got plenty," Cody assured him, "but if it gets colder, we'll be wanting some hot chocolate."

"That would be all right. Did you bring any?"

"Nope."

"Hey, guys, we're almost finished!" Larry called out as he bounce-passed the ball to Cody. "Let's go over a couple of fast-break drills again."

"Fast break?" Jeremiah protested. "We're only playing half-court basketball. What do we want with a fast break?"

"Didn't we do everything on your list?" Cody asked.

"Yeah, but that doesn't mean we have to quit."

"I'm done . . . finished . . . through . . . time to relax," Cody declared.

"Wait! Just a little more. One more drill. This is a new one. It will really improve our skills," Larry persisted.

"If I improve anymore, I'll have to skip high school and go straight to the NBA," Jeremiah boasted. "I'm with Cody. I'm out of here."

"Free throws." Larry ignored their protests. "Let's each shoot fifty more."

"We're through, Larry. Really through," Cody maintained.

"Twenty-five?"

"Forget it, Lewis. It's Gatorade and Double-Stuffed Oreo time!" Jeremiah headed to the barn door.

"You brought Oreos?" Cody asked.

"Hey, guys! Wait . . . wait! Let's each just shoot free throws until we make ten in a row. How about it?"

Jeremiah looked over at Cody. "What kind of goodies did you bring?"

"I brought some homemade chocolate chip cookies and a box of powdered sugar doughnuts for breakfast."

"Hey, Townie," Larry called, "you can go first. Really. Come on! If we get going right away, we could probably finish before dark."

"We're finished now, Larry. You can stay out here if you want, but it will be a lot warmer up there in the loft."

Jeremiah yanked on the big wooden handle of the barn's front door. "Hey, what's the secret here, Cody? How come this door won't open?"

"I don't know. . . . Give a good jerk on it; maybe it's starting to sag," Cody urged.

Jeremiah tugged and yanked. "I think it's locked. Maybe it accidentally locked when we closed it."

"It can't accidentally lock. That wooden bar has to be slid into the brackets from the inside. Who closed that door anyway?" Cody pondered.

"I did!"

The voice from above sounded imposing, victorious, and feminine.

All three boys strained to look up at the open door to the hay loft.

"Feather!" It was a chorus of surprise and amazement.

"How sweet. You all still remember my name—even though I wasn't invited to a team practice and overnighter."

"Feather, you can't—can't be out here!" Cody stammered.

"Well, I am here, and you can't make me go home. In fact, you can't even get in the barn unless I let you in."

"Feather, you can't . . . It's just that . . . Come on, Feather, let us in the barn!" Cody called out.

"Not until you promise that I get to be a part of everything."

"You can't stay, Feather."

"Why not?"

"We've gone through that before. It's not proper for a girl to be camping out with boys when there's no parents around."

"What's the matter? You guys afraid of me?"

"That's not it!"

"Well, you ought to be scared. I've got the pitchfork! Hey, these Oreos are good. Did you ever take two double-stuffed ones, take off the top and jam them together? Quadruple-stuffed Oreos."

"You're eating my cookies!" Jeremiah hollered.

"Feather, does your mother know you're out here?" Cody questioned.

"Of course she does. She said if you don't let me come

to the overnighter, we'll have the ACLU sue you for sex discrimination."

Larry dropped the basketball. "Sue us for what?"

"You've got to be kidding," Cody groaned.

"Well, I did make up the part about suing. But my mother said I could come out here."

"But this is a boys' thing," Jeremiah tried to explain.

"Not anymore. If you want, I can toss down the black cookies after I've licked the filling out."

"Oh, yuuck!" Jeremiah wailed.

"I wouldn't mind if you pitched my sweatshirt down," Cody put in. "It's getting cold out here."

"Oh, I'm afraid I couldn't do that—not until you invite me to stay."

"I can't do that," Cody protested.

"Well, good night, fellas. Sleep well. I'll see you in the morning. Think I'll close these doors now."

"Wait," Cody shouted. "Look . . . wait."

Lord, how did I get in this bind? We can't call Mom to come pick up Feather. We don't even have our bikes here. Her mother said she could come out. . . . I guess we can walk back to town and leave her out here by herself, but she might be in more danger out here alone if something strange is going on over at Eureka's.

How come everything seems easier when you talk about it than when you try to do it?

"I'm waiting, Cody!" Feather persisted. "Hey, whose GameBoy is this?"

"That's mine!" Larry shouted.

"NBA Jam? The only game you brought was NBA Jam?" she complained.

"Don't mess around with that!" Larry called out. Then he turned to Cody. "Hurry up and think of something. I'm getting cold."

"Look," Cody began, "this whole thing isn't my idea, but I guess we've got to do the right thing under the circumstances. So, Feather, you can stay, but you'll have to sleep in the tack room. It's nice in there. It has an electric light and a woodstove if you need one. What do you say?"

"Since when are you the one making the decisions?"

"It's my barn."

"Not at the moment it isn't."

"You know what I mean."

There was a long pause. "I get to stay up here and help watch until it's time to go to bed."

Cody glanced at Jeremiah and Larry. They were both rubbing their arms to keep warm.

"Okay, you can stay with us. But you have to promise to ride home in the morning before my mother picks us up."

"All right. Do you promise me you'll let me stay, Cody Clark?"

"I promise."

"Open the door," Jeremiah hollered. "I need my jacket."

"And do you promise, Cody Clark, you won't treat me mean and play tricks on me and not let me be a part of things?"

"Yeah, I promise."

"Open up!" Larry banged on the rough wooden door.

"And you've got to promise—," Feather began again.

"All right, he'll do it!" Larry shouted. "I've gone to weddings that didn't take this long. Open the door!"

"Not if you're going to use that tone of voice!"

Larry beat on the door two more times. "Please!" he begged.

All three boys huddled by the big front door until they heard the two-by-four brace slide back out of the way.

Feather appeared, wrapped in a coat made out of a Hudson's Bay Company blanket. The red, blue, green, and yellow stripes of the points ran horizontally around her like wide belts on the cream-colored wool.

All four scrambled up to the loft where the boys pulled on their jackets, and Cody scooted some bales of hay around by the open loft door to act as a windbreak. Sprawling on the hay, Jeremiah and the bag of double-stuffed cookies took first watch with the binoculars pointed at Eureka Blaine's pasture.

Larry settled in a corner with a hooded red Indiana University sweatshirt pulled over his head and the GameBoy in his hands. Cody downed a blue Gatorade and then settled in to carving on a stick with his pocket knife.

"Is that all you brought to eat?" he asked Feather.

"I have plenty."

"You can have some of ours. We brought a bunch of stuff."

"I *like* carrot strips and homemade peach tea. It's one of my favorite snacks," she informed him.

"Really?"

She spoke softly as if she didn't want Jeremiah and

Larry to hear. "Look, it's not real easy to make a bunch of snacks when you don't have a refrigerator or freezer at home."

"Feather, I've been wanting to ask you a question . . . but, you know, you don't have to answer it if you don't want to," Cody began.

"What?"

"Well . . . living out in a tepee—no electricity or running water or plumbing—and stuff . . ."

"What about it?"

"Do you really like living like that? I mean, is it fun? Or do you sort of wish you lived like everybody else?"

She looked him straight in the eye. He thought she looked sad. Tears started to puddle in the corners. "We get along quite well, thank you."

Her answer sounded like a simulated voice from a computer game.

"I've always had brothers and always lived in town where there were other kids," Cody allowed. "My folks built our house when they got married. Of course they've added on some, but they've always lived right there."

"I've never spent two Christmases in the same place," she admitted.

"Never?"

"No. But my dad says one day we'll get a big log house built and never move again. I'll have a room with a door on it."

"Didn't you have a house in Oregon before you moved here?"

"It had one bedroom, so I slept on the couch in the living room. But it wasn't a very nice house. One time we lived in an old railroad car. . . . That was pretty cool, really."

Feather wasn't looking at him. She wiped her eyes on her blanket jacket.

"Well, I think I'm going to ask the Lord to give you a place to live where you have your own room with a door, and you get to stay there more than one Christmas, and you have lots of friends close by to visit and do things with."

Neither said a word for several moments. The only noise was an occasional beep from Larry's GameBoy and a crunch from Jeremiah's direction as another Oreo found its eternal rest.

"You take that talking to the Lord stuff seriously, don't you?" she finally asked.

"It's not a game, Feather. He's real."

"Yeah, my mom hears voices, too."

"That's not the same thing. I mean, I talk to God a lot, but when He talks to me, it's usually through the Bible or maybe giving me a little nudge in my conscience as to what I ought to do. I don't hear voices."

"Sometimes I get to wishing I had something real like that," Feather acknowledged.

"You could, you know. Jesus just waits for us to make up our minds about Him."

"No, it's not that easy for me. Mom says I can't choose a religion until after I'm twenty-one."

"Why?"

"She says there's so much propaganda floating around that a person needs to wait until they can study everything for themselves."

"I'm sure glad my folks didn't make me wait. I would have missed lots of years of talking to the Lord."

Feather shook her head. "I've never been around anyone like you before."

Cody was glad it was almost dark inside the barn because he knew he was beginning to blush. "Well, I, eh," he stammered, "I guess I haven't ever been around someone like me either."

"Hey, look at this!" Jeremiah hollered from his perch behind the hay bale fence at the outside opening of the loft.

Cody jumped to his feet and scurried to the door. "What is it, Townie?"

Jeremiah, his lips almost black with Oreo crumbs, handed Cody the binoculars. "Look over there!"

"Where?"

"Toward the road." Jeremiah pointed. "Is that cool or what?"

Ten

I don't see anything over there but the moon coming up,"
Cody confessed.

"It's awesome, isn't it?" Jeremiah grinned.

"That's what you got all excited about?" Disgust
showed on Larry's face. "You made me miss that basket."

"Are you winning?" Feather asked him.

"Oh . . . yeah."

"What's the score?" she pressed.

Larry looked down at his GameBoy and mumbled,
"Eh, it's ninety-seven to fourteen."

"You're winning by over eighty points!"

"I'm having a good game."

"It sounds boring," she observed.

"Oh, no, it's fun . . . really."

Cody took his turn at the loft door. Jeremiah dug
through the goodies for some potato chips. Over the next
two hours the conversation turned from basketball . . . to

food . . . to music . . . to school teachers . . . to rodeo . . . and back to basketball.

"I think my batteries are wearing out," Larry announced.

"I think Townie's went out a long time ago." Cody motioned to the sleeping Jeremiah. "Maybe it's time we all went to sleep." He turned to Feather. "Did you bring a flashlight?"

"Yes."

"Well, I'll . . . you know . . . I'll go help you set up the tack room," he stammered.

"I'm perfectly capable of taking care of myself," she huffed.

"Yeah, I know, but I thought maybe I'd throw the bolt on the front door of the barn."

Feather gathered up her things and headed toward the ladder. "I know why you're coming down," she said quietly.

Cody followed her down the ladder with a flashlight lighting each step. "Why?"

"Because you feel it's somehow your duty to look after me. I'm the poor, helpless girl, and you're the strong, protective boy—right?"

"I guess that's sort of it, but you aren't helpless, and I'm not all that brave. I suppose that insults you."

"No, not really." She spoke so softly Cody could hardly hear.

"Well, I don't mean it to be insulting. I just try real hard to do what I think is right. Sometimes I really blow it."

"I said, I didn't mind you acting that way!"

"You did? Oh . . . yeah, good." Cody squeezed past

Feather, reached into the tack room, and turned on the light. "It's the only electricity out here. Sometimes we use this room for calving. When that happens, Dad just sleeps out here. That's why that cot is over there. You can just move the saddle to that barrel if you'd like. Is everything okay?" he asked.

"It's big! It will be great."

"Lock the door after I leave," Cody instructed.

"Why?"

"Because it will make me feel better," he replied. "Besides, you like rooms with doors."

"Yeah. You're right. Good night, Cody." She looked down at her shoes when she talked. "Thanks for caring about me."

"Good night, Feather girl." He didn't have the nerve to look back at her.

The plan was to trade off watching out the loft door in case there was a nocturnal prowler at Eureka Blaine's. But the plan didn't last long. By 11:30 Larry Lewis, Jeremiah Yellowboy, Cody Clark—and Feather Trailer-Hobbs were all fast asleep.

Cody backed the long-legged buckskin quarter horse into the far corner of the box. With his left hand he screwed his cowboy hat down tight. The coiled nylon rope was tucked under his right arm, the pigging string clamped in his mouth. He built a loop and tried to ignore the 18,000 cheering, screaming fans that had crammed into Thomas and Mack Arena for the National Finals Rodeo.

The calf in the chute bent its head to the left. Cody waited for it to get straightened around.

The Beaver's in with an 8.0, and Fred has 7.9. I've got to have 7.8, or I won't take home the gold buckle.

"This is it, Pancake. Don't you break that barrier. We're goin' to put him down quick, wrap once, and pray."

The white-faced Hereford calf turned his head and stared at the far end of the arena. Cody nodded his head. . . . The gate flew open. . . . The calf bolted. . . . Pancake flew toward the rope barrier. . . . The loop flew around Cody's head only once and then sailed across the dirt arena to settle down on the calf's neck.

Pancake put on the brakes. Cody leaped off the right side, letting out the slack. In a blur, he was down the rope, had flanked the calf, wrapped once and tied a hooey. Then slowly he walked back to the horse and remounted. He rode Pancake forward, giving slack to the rope and waited.

Out of the corner of his eye, he thought he saw 7.7 flash on the scoreboard, but he didn't dare look until the six-second wait was over. Suddenly the calf let go with a frantic kick.

"No!" Cody shouted.

"Yes!"

"No!"

"Cody? I need you to come look!"

It wasn't a rodeo voice. It wasn't a man's voice.

It was a woman. A girl. A girl close by, and she was saying something urgent. Suddenly the calf was gone. The horse was gone. The arena was gone.

"Cody, wake up! I need you to check something out. Please wake up!"

His eyes flipped open to a barn filled with predawn light and the sound of a soft voice.

"Feather?" he mumbled.

"Cody, come here and check this out!"

"What's happening? Wait, you're supposed to be in the tack room. How long have you been up here?" he quizzed.

"Are you going to get up and come see what's going on or not?"

"What time is it?"

"Your watch says 4:30."

"In the morning?"

"Yeah, is your watch right?"

Cody realized that his arm with his watch was still down in his sleeping bag.

"How do you know what my watch says?"

"Get up, Clark, or the cops will be gone."

"What cops?" Cody pulled himself out of his sleeping bag. He was still wearing exactly what he had on the night before, except for his basketball shoes. Larry and Jeremiah were sprawled on the hay sound asleep. "Did you say cops?" In his stocking feet, Cody staggered over to where Feather stood gazing east in the predawn light.

"Yeah, it looks like a roadblock or something out at County Line Road. See?" She pointed to flashing lights on two black and white vehicles that blocked off the gravel road back to the ranch.

"Oh, man," Cody moaned, "this is it."

"I'll bet they located the pickup, and it was used in

some crime, and they're sealing off the area to investigate," Feather surmised.

"What about the limo?" he asked.

"Maybe that was the Mafia."

"In north-central Idaho?"

"Well, there must be some kind of organized crime around here."

"I don't think anything within 200 miles is organized."

"Except for Larry." She grinned.

Cody dashed over and woke Jeremiah and Larry. Soon all four stood at the loft opening and gazed out at the flashing lights.

"Should we go down there and ask them what's going on?" Jeremiah asked.

"If we go down there, they'll probably just tell us to go home, and we'll never find out what's happening," Larry cautioned. "Let's just sit here and see what happens next."

"I wonder if they're waiting for Bruce," Cody pondered.

Feather crawled up on a bale of hay and sat down. "Who?"

"You know, the name on that piece of cardboard in that picture," Cody explained.

"Who wants a doughnut?" Jeremiah rummaged through the goodies sack. All four perched on bales of hay and watched the flashing lights at County Line Road.

"Whoa! Look at that big white semi!" Cody pointed to the road.

"And a white travel home . . . and a big white van." Larry stood up and walked a little closer to the open door.

"A crime investigation team. That's what it is. They can

haul a lot of gear in those rigs. They're probably looking for a dead body," Feather put in.

"Maybe those pictures we found will help them," Jeremiah suggested.

"You think I ought to take them the photos?"

"Yeah. Who knows, maybe there'll be a reward or something," Feather spouted.

"Where are they going?"

"Look! They stopped at Eureka's corrals! I knew it. We were right. There's something suspicious about that old truck. Didn't I say from the beginning there was something funny about it being out there?" Cody blabbed on.

"I wonder why they need a travel home?" Feather probed.

"Wait . . . they're pulling equipment out of the truck. Let me use the binoculars!" Larry shouted. He grabbed them out of Jeremiah's hand and put them up to his eyes. "It's a crime investigation team, all right. They're pulling out the cameras."

"Really? Let me see." Jeremiah wrestled him for control of the binoculars.

"Oh, no! That pickup has our fingerprints all over it!" Larry moaned.

"And mine are on the inside!" Feather shrieked. "They'll know that I was inside the truck."

"Hey, relax. We didn't do anything. We aren't guilty of anything. Don't panic," Cody reassured them. "It looks like they're trying to figure out where to set the cameras. They have more than one. Let me take a look." He reached over and took the binoculars from Jeremiah. "It looks like they're setting the cameras over by the fence. The angle they have toward the pickup will be just the same as the one in the 'Bruce' photo."

"This is so totally cool!" Jeremiah reveled.

"I've got to go take them these photos. They might be part of the evidence or something."

"What if they arrest you—for stealing the film?" Larry cautioned.

"They won't arrest me. Come on," Cody insisted, "you guys come with me."

"Why?" Larry gulped. "We didn't steal any film."

"Neither did I." Cody pulled on his basketball shoes. "Are you guys coming with me or not?"

Within minutes the Lewis and Clark Squad left the barn and hiked toward the gravel road. Cody was in the lead, sporting his National Finals Rodeo sweatshirt. Feather on his left side had donned her blanket coat. Jeremiah on his right wore a Bulls jacket. Larry, in University of Indiana red, trailed behind—dribbling the basketball.

They had just crossed the gravel road when a security guard dressed in dark blue shouted at them. "Stop! You can't go in there!"

All four froze in place and waited for the man to reach them.

"Where did you kids come from?" he demanded.

"From over at my barn." Cody motioned behind him.

"Someone lives over there?" the man asked.

"No, we were just camping out."

"Well, there's no one allowed here. You kids go on back over to your barn."

Jeremiah and Larry turned to go. Cody looked at the man and then over at Feather, who stayed right by his side.

"But I've got to feed the stock," Cody explained.

"You've got to do what?"

"Mr. Blaine, who owns this place, hired me to feed the horses. I do it every day." Cody studied the pasture where it looked as if a dozen people were working.

"What's your name?" the man asked.

"Cody Clark."

"I'll check the roster. You kids stay right here." He spun around and hustled over to the big fifteen-passenger white van.

"What did he mean, check the roster?" Jeremiah asked.

"What's that thing?" Larry pointed to four men jockeying a huge fanlike object out into the pasture.

"It looks like a wind machine."

"Why does anyone want to make wind?"

The security guard came back. "Yep, Cody, you're on the list. Go ahead and feed your animals, but you have to stay out of the pasture."

"Eh, thanks. Come on, guys, let's go—"

"Oh, no! They can't go. You're the only one on the list."

"But these are my friends, and they help me feed the—"

"Sorry, but if their names are not on the list, they can't go in until after the shoot."

"Shoot?" Larry croaked. "You're going to shoot? Maybe I'll just wait over at the barn."

Cody reached into the pocket of his sweatshirt.

"Mister, can you ask somebody if these pictures belong to anyone over here. We found a roll of film and had them developed, you know, just to see who they belonged to."

"You found the film!" the guard shouted. "You got them developed?"

"Yeah, see I wanted to—"

"Let me have those. Wait here—all of you, wait here."

The man went over to the corral fence and called to the man who was supervising setting up two large cameras.

"Cody, look." Feather pointed to the travel home. "What's the name on the door under that silver star?"

"Bruce!"

The security guard returned with a short balding man who wore a green sweater and a Riviera Country Club golf hat on his head.

"You kids found this film out here?" he asked.

"Eh, yes, sir," Cody confirmed. "Down by that concrete tombstone. We didn't know who it belonged to, so we thought . . . you know, if we had it developed, we could tell who to give it to. We weren't stealing it. I'm sorry."

"Sorry?" The man smiled. "Son, you just saved me at least a thousand dollars. This is great!" He waved at the security guard. "Jerry, tell Bruce we'll be ready to shoot in thirty minutes max."

"What about these kids?"

"Give them passes for all day, and that includes a meal ticket with the caterer."

"You heard the man. Here, wear these and no one will hassle you."

Cody looked at the clip-on tag: "Day Pass—All Rights—Buena Ventura Films."

"Just remember to stay out of the pasture where they're taping, and when you hear someone holler, 'Quiet,' for pete's sake, be quiet." The guard turned toward the big white van.

"Hey, mister, what's going on here anyway?" Feather asked.

He spun around. "Don't you know? We're filming a commercial."

"What kind?" Jeremiah asked.

"Pizza Palace," the man called back. Then he stepped behind the van.

"A commercial?"

"What about the murder?" Feather asked.

"Did you say murder?"

"Eh . . . nothing," she gulped.

"Why are they making a commercial way out here?" Cody drawled.

"Haven't you seen those spots: 'Going where no pizza has ever gone before!'" Larry laughed.

"Pizza for the whole planet," Jeremiah continued. "You know, those great commercials where Bruce Baxter is all over the world eating—"

"Bruce!" It was a perfectly timed quartet.

"Bruce Baxter is in that travel home?" Feather swooned. "I saw him in *A Month of Sundays*. Did you see that movie? Oh, man, this is so awesome! Bruce Baxter! He makes Brad Pitt look like a boring wimp!"

"I can't believe this! Do you know that Bruce Baxter

has court-side seats at every Laker game? Not that I like the Lakers, of course," Larry announced.

"This is cool. Cody, my man," Jeremiah rambled, "let's go over there and sit on the rail of the corral and watch everything!"

"I've got to feed the horses," Cody reminded them. "Save me a place to sit. I'll hurry!"

"I'll come help you," Feather offered.

"Eh . . . okay. You two go save us a spot."

Cody was surprised to find out how much Feather knew about taking care of horses. The chores were soon finished, and they raced back to the corrals to join Jeremiah and Larry.

"Did anything happen?" Cody asked.

"Did you see Bruce Baxter yet?" Feather quizzed.

"No, nothing's happened except that they've moved those cameras a dozen different times," Larry informed them.

"Baxter hasn't come out yet," Jeremiah added.

All four sat on the fence and stared at a crew that seemed to be in a hurry. The sky was clear, but the sun was still not up yet. Everyone seemed to be in place. Waiting for something.

Finally, the door of the travel home opened. A lady with a comb in her hand stepped out first, followed by a tall, broad-shouldered man with close-cut hair.

"That's him!" Feather giggled. "That's really Bruce Baxter!"

"This is unreal," Jeremiah whispered. "I keep thinking I'll wake up and it's just a dream."

"Hey, we're supposed to keep quiet, guys," Cody cautioned.

"Not until they yell, 'Quiet.'"

The man with the golf cap talked to Bruce Baxter near the old pickup.

"He's pointing over here," Feather said.

"Maybe he told Baxter about the film we found."

Feather reached over and put her hand on top of Cody's. He started to pull it back and then hesitated. "Thanks for letting me stay in the barn last night. I would have died if I had missed all this. I'm going to be an actor someday, you know." She pulled her hand back.

"Mr. Clark!" The man in the golf cap was waving for him to join them.

"He wants you to go over there!" Larry shouted.

Cody slipped down off the fence and slowly made his way through the herd of adults clustered around the old pickup.

"Cody," the man in the green sweater began, "Bruce just had a great idea for a script change. We've decided we want to have a kid sitting up on the fender of this old pickup, holding a piece of pizza. There won't be any lines to say or anything. If we end up wanting to use those scenes, we'll need some release forms signed by your parents, and you'll get paid a little."

Cody stared up at Bruce Baxter, who looked even taller than six-foot-four. "You want me to be in a commercial with you?"

"Any one of you kids will do." Baxter smiled. "I heard

you were the one that developed and delivered that lost roll of film. So what do you say?"

"Does it, eh, does it matter to you which one of us is in the commercial?"

"Nope. But we're going to get started in six minutes."

"I'll be right back!" Cody took off on a dead run back to the corral fence.

"What did they say?" Feather shouted as he approached.

"They want you to be in a commercial with Bruce Baxter."

"Me?" Feather gasped. "They want me?"

"Yeah, come on. They said your mom would have to sign some release papers later, and you might even get paid for it."

"Oh, sure," Larry moaned, "they always want the girls!"

"Just the pretty ones," Cody blurted out and was instantly flooded with embarrassment. Feather jumped down off the corral fence and ran, hand in hand, with Cody over to the pickup.

"We decided that Feather should be in the commercial. She's a lot better at that sort of thing than I am," Cody announced.

"She'll do just fine," Baxter said and then resumed a conversation with the man in the golf hat.

"They didn't ask for me?" she whispered.

"That was my idea," Cody admitted. "Have fun!"

Feather suddenly threw her arms around Cody and kissed him on the cheek.

"Whoa! Hold it right there, partner!" Baxter boomed out. "No one's allowed to kiss the leading lady on my sets except for me. It's in my contract."

"Really?" Feather gulped.

"That's right, darlin'. Now let Suzy do a little makeup on you, and we'll be ready to shoot."

Feather started to follow the lady with the comb over to the travel home. Then she stopped, turned, and looked back at Cody.

"How come you let me be the one to do this?" she asked.

"It seemed like the thing the Lord wanted me to do." Cody shrugged.

"Would you teach me how to talk to Him sometime?"

"Yep."

She trailed the lady to the travel home. When she got to the step next to the door, she turned and glanced back at Cody.

He gave her two thumbs up.

The morning sun spotlighted her wide smile and sparkled off her eyes. Cody couldn't decide if it was a twinkle . . . or a tear.

Or both.

For a list of other books by Stephen Bly
or information regarding speaking engagements
write:

Stephen Bly
Winchester, Idaho 83555